Camp Club Girls

Sydney's
OUTER
BANKS
BLAST

© 2010 by Barbour Publishing, Inc.

Edited by Jeanette Littleton.

ISBN 978-1-60260-291-5

Scripture taken from the New American Standard Bible, © 1960, 1962, 1963, 1968, 1971, 1972, 1973, 1975, 1977, 1995 by The Lockman Foundation. Used by permission

Scripture taken from the HOLY BIBLE, NEW INTERNATIONAL VERSION®. NIV®. Copyright © 1973, 1978, 1984 by International Bible Society. Used by permission of Zondervan. All rights reserved.

This book is a work of fiction. Names, characters, places, and incidents are either products of the author's imagination or used fictitiously. Any similarity to actual people, organizations, and/or events is purely coincidental.

Cover design: Thinkpen Design

Published by Barbour Publishing, Inc., P.O. Box 719, Uhrichsville, Ohio 44683, www.barbourbooks.com

Our mission is to publish and distribute inspirational products offering exceptional value and biblical encouragement to the masses.

Member of the
Evangelical Christian
Publishers Association

Printed in the United States of America.
Dickinson Press; Grand Rapids, MI; May 2010; D10002361

Camp Club Girls

Sydney's
OUTER
BANKS
BLAST

Jean Fischer

BARBOUR
PUBLISHING

Sydney's Ghost Story

"It wasn't a UFO," said Sydney Lincoln as she and Bailey walked along the beach. "There's a logical explanation for it."

Bailey Chang disagreed. "I looked out at the ocean at two o'clock this morning, and there it was. It had red flashing lights, and it was hovering over the water. It spun around and around, and then *poof*, it was gone. It was a UFO!"

Sydney bent and picked up some small stones from the sand. "What were you doing up at two o'clock?" she asked as she walked to the water's edge.

"I couldn't sleep in a strange bed," Bailey told her.

Sydney waited a few seconds before skipping a stone across the waves. "I think what you saw was just a coastguard training exercise, or something."

"It was a UFO," Bailey insisted. "I'm sure of it."

"I don't believe in UFOs," said Sydney skipping another stone. "Anyway, I'm glad your parents let you come. Ever since camp, I've wanted to show you the ocean."

Sydney had invited her friend Bailey to spend a week at her grandparents' beach house on the Outer Banks of

North Carolina. Sydney loved to escape the activity of her home in Washington DC for the peace and quiet of the long, narrow string of barrier islands that separated the Atlantic Ocean from several sounds off the edge of North Carolina.

Bailey was always willing to accept an invitation to anywhere. She couldn't wait to leave her hometown of Peoria, Illinois, and see the world. Now, in the early morning sunshine, Bailey was getting her first taste of the salty ocean air as she and Sydney walked together through the sand.

"It's not exactly what I expected," Bailey said.

She had imagined that the Atlantic Ocean would look vastly different from the huge Great Lake that bordered her home state. In fact, the ocean *was* very different—much larger and far grander—but just not as different as Bailey had hoped for. She was often disappointed when real life didn't match up to her imagination.

"The ocean sort of looks like Lake Michigan," she said. "Lake Michigan also has waves, and it's so big that you can't see to the other side."

She picked up a handful of sand and let it sift through her fingers. "This beach looks like it's not taken care of. In Chicago, a tractor pulls a machine that combs the sand and keeps it nice and clean. There aren't weeds and stuff sticking up, like here. And they test the water to make sure it's not polluted."

Sydney kicked at the sugar-fine sand with her bare feet.

"Nobody tests the water here," she said. "It's clean. I swim in it all the time." She waded into the ocean a few yards offshore.

"Come on!" she told Bailey. "Check it out."

Bailey hesitated. "What about jellyfish and sharks?" she asked.

"If I see some, I'll introduce you," Sydney said, joking.

Bailey rolled the legs of her khaki pants over her knees. Then she tiptoed into the breakers. All at once, she felt the world between her toes as she imagined thousands of miles between herself and the nearest shore.

Sydney and Bailey had met at Discovery Lake Camp where they bunked in Cabin 12 with four other girls: Alexis Howell from Sacramento, California; Elizabeth Anderson, from Amarillo, Texas; McKenzie Phillips, from White Sulphur Springs, Montana; and Kate Oliver, from Philadelphia, Pennsylvania. The Camp Club Girls, as they called themselves, were the best of friends. They loved to explore, and they'd become quite good at solving mysteries together. When they weren't at summer camp, the girls kept in touch by chatting on their Camp Club Girls Web site, sending instant messages and e-mails, and even by phone and cell phones.

"I still think it was a UFO," said Bailey splashing in the water. "I'm sure that it wasn't an airplane, so what else could it be?"

7

"Oh, I don't know," Sydney answered. She added with a fond grin, "Maybe your imagination?"

As the girls waded and splashed in the water, only one other person was in sight, and he kept a very safe distance away from them.

"Who's that?" Bailey asked, pointing a shell she'd picked up towards the boy.

"I think his name is Drake or something," Sydney said. "He's kind of different. I see him alone on the beach sometimes. But it seems whenever people show up, he just kind of disappears."

"He's about your age, it looks like," Bailey said, squinting to see him better. "Looks like he's kind of cute, too."

"I don't know how anyone can tell if he's cute or not," Sydney said. "He always keeps his head down, digging around in the sand."

"What's he looking for? Shells?" Bailey asked.

"I dunno," Sydney said, shrugging. "It seems whenever he picks up something, it's bigger than shells, though. Some friends of mine who live here all the time, the Kessler twins, say he's a relative of the Wright brothers. Remember where we drove across the causeway? The Wright brothers did their famous flying around there."

"Well, that's neat! To be related to the Wright brothers!" Bailey exclaimed.

Sydney waded out of the ocean and stood on the shore. She watched Bailey scoop water into her hands, smell it, and then carefully stick her tongue in the water.

"It tastes sort of like potatoes boiled in salt water," Bailey observed.

"Whatever you say," Sydney answered. Her wet legs were caked up to her knees with sand, and against her chocolate-colored skin, the sand looked like knee socks. She bent over and brushed it off. "Let's take a walk up the shore," she said.

Bailey hurried out of the water and fell into step alongside her friend. The boy saw them coming, and he walked quickly on ahead of them. After they had gone around a hundred feet along the beach, Bailey's right foot landed on something hard. "Ouch!" she said.

Sydney, who was a few steps ahead, stopped and turned around to see what was the matter. "What's wrong?" she asked, "Crab got your toe?"

Bailey jumped. "Where?"

"Where what?"

"Where's a crab?"

"I didn't see a crab," Sydney answered. "I just wondered if you got pinched by one."

"No," Bailey told her. "I stepped on something."

Sydney explored the sand where Bailey stood. "Do you have crabs in Lake Michigan?"

"We have crayfish," Bailey answered. "I don't know if they live on the beach, or if they're just bait that fishermen leave behind, but I've seen them there a couple of times.

They're brown and ugly, and they have big claws. They kind of look like lobsters."

Sydney saw a white bump protruding from the sand. She reached down and pulled it up. It was a long, slender bone, a rib bone, maybe, from a wild animal, or possibly left from a beachfront barbeque. Tiny bits of dried flesh clung to its underside. Sydney held it up and showed it to Bailey. "This is what you stepped on," she said. "It's a bone."

"Eeeewwww!" said Bailey. "Where do you think it came from?"

"Oh, I don't know," Sydney teased. "Maybe from the body of an old sailor who died at sea. They call part of the Outer Banks the Graveyard of the Atlantic, you know."

"Eeeewwww!" Bailey said again. "Are there really dead sailors floating around out there?"

"Oh sure," Sydney said matter-of-factly. "Not to mention the ones from the ghost ship."

Bailey shuddered. "Ghost ship! What ghost ship?"

"The *Carroll A. Deering*," Sydney replied. She tossed the bone into the water and walked on with Bailey at her side.

"The story of the *Carroll A. Deering* is really spooky," Sydney went on. "I don't know if I should tell it to you. You might be too afraid." She looked at Bailey and grinned.

"I will not!" Bailey protested. "I'm not scared of anything."

"Well, okay then," Sydney answered. "But if you can't sleep tonight, don't blame me."

She stopped and picked up a stick at the ocean's edge. Frothy, white fingers of water washed across the beach, scrabbling at the firm wet sand. Sydney used the stick to write BEWARE OF UFOs on the gritty, light tan canvas. Then she tossed the stick back to the ocean. The girls walked on leaving two sets of footprints behind them.

"The *Carroll A. Deering* was a tall ship, a schooner," Sydney began. "Pirates used several types of sailing ships. The ships they used had to be fast and strong. The *Carroll A. Deering* was bigger than most schooners. It had five tall masts with billowy sails—"

"I know exactly what you're talking about," Bailey interrupted. "Those kind of tall ships came to Navy Pier in Chicago last summer. Of course, they weren't old ones. They were only made to look like the old ones. Mom, Dad, my sister, Trina, and I went to check them out. They looked really old, and we even got to sail on one of them out on the lake."

"Cool," said Sydney. "So, since you've been *on* a tall ship, you can imagine what it was like to be a sailor on the *Carroll A. Deering* back in 1921. Imagine that it's the middle of winter. Some coastguardsmen are looking out at the ocean, sort of like we are now. They're about a hundred miles south of here near the Cape Hatteras Lighthouse, down by Diamond Shoals."

"What's that?" asked Bailey. She carefully stepped through the sand watching for bones and other hidden objects.

"What's what?"

"Diamond Shoals."

"It's a bunch of sandbars just off the coast of the Outer Banks, down at the southern end," Sydney replied. "Anyhow, that's where they saw it."

"The ghost ship?" Bailey asked. Just saying the words sent a little shiver up her spine.

"The ghost ship—the *Carroll A. Deering*," Sydney answered. "There she was, half washed up on one of the shoals, with her sails still opened wide and flapping in the wind. The ocean was pushing at her from behind. Her prow, that's the front end of the ship, was scraping against some rocks in the sand. *Scrape. . .scrape. . .*" As Sydney said the words, she brushed the tips of her fingers along the side of Bailey's arm.

"Stop it!" Bailey said. "You're spooking me out."

"I thought nothing scared you," Sydney answered. "Maybe I shouldn't tell you the rest."

A seagull swept over Bailey's head. It dove and snatched a small fish out of the ocean. "Go on," she said tentatively. "I want to hear."

"It was a foggy, cold, misty morning," Sydney continued, "and the sea was rough. The men of the Coast Guard knew it would be really hard getting to the wreck, but they had to, because they knew that the crew was in danger. So they got into their heavy wooden rowboat, and they rowed through the boiling waves toward the shoals."

"But it was the middle of winter," said Bailey.

"So?" Sydney asked.

"You said that the waves were boiling, and if that's true, it was summertime. You're making this up, aren't you?"

"Bailey!" Sydney protested. "It was a figure of speech. The sea was rough. The waves were rolling *like* boiling water. That's all. The ocean never gets hot enough to boil, and this is a true story. You can ask anyone on the Outer Banks, and they'll tell you—it's true."

Bailey stopped in the sand and let the edge of the ocean tickle her toes. "Okay," she conceded.

"So anyway," said Sydney. "They got into their big rowboat, and they rowed out to the *Carroll A. Deering*. When they reached her, they climbed up onto her deck."

"How'd they climb onto it?" Bailey wondered. "Did they have a ladder? Weren't the waves too rough?"

"I don't know. They were the coastguardsmen, and they know how to climb up on decks and stuff." Sydney swatted at a deerfly that landed on her elbow. "And when they got up on the deck, it was eerily quiet except for the waves lapping at the sides of the ship and that awful *scrape. . . scrape. . . .*"

Bailey pulled away as Sydney's long fingers reached for her arm.

"Ahoy!" Sydney yelled.

Bailey jumped.

"Did I scare you?"

13

"I just didn't expect you to yell, that's all," said Bailey. "And why did you?"

"That's what the Coast Guard yelled," Sydney said. "They stood on the deck, and they yelled, 'Ahoy there! Is anyone here?' But nobody answered. So they searched the deserted deck, and the only sounds they heard were the echo of their own footsteps."

"Don't forget the waves and the scraping," Bailey interjected.

"And the waves and the scraping," said Sydney. "And after looking around the top deck, they went down into the center of the ship, and then they opened the door to the crew's quarters. And do you know what they found?" Sydney stopped. She looked at Bailey and grinned.

"Stop playing with me," Bailey said. "What did they find?"

"Nobody," said Sydney. "There was no one there. The beds had all been slept in, and everything was shipshape, except that eleven crewmen and their stuff were gone."

"Gone?" Bailey wondered.

"Just like that. Disappeared. Then the coastguardsmen went to check out the galley. There was food standing out like someone had been preparing a meal, only nobody had eaten anything. The table was all set with plates, cups, and silverware, but nothing had been touched. So the men checked out the officers' quarters next. The beds had been slept in, and the officers' boots were on the floor next to their beds, but nobody was there. Their personal stuff was gone and so was the ship's log, the navigating instruments, all of it—gone."

"So where did everybody go?" Bailey asked.

"Nobody knows," Sydney answered. "It's a big mystery around here. It was like they vanished into thin air. The sailors were never found. The shoals are near enough to shore that something should have washed up, if not their bodies, then some of their belongings, but nothing ever did—"

Sydney's story was interrupted by a powerful, rhythmic noise. All at once, a swirling cloud of sand covered Sydney and Bailey as something huge and brown rushed past them.

Bailey screamed. She gripped Sydney's arm. "A horse!" she cried.

In the swirling dust, she saw a muscular, brown stallion galloping on ahead of them. Its black mane stood on end as it raced against the wind.

Sydney caught her breath. The horse had frightened her as much as it had Bailey. She wondered if God was having a good laugh, getting even with her for trying to scare Bailey with the ghost story of the *Carroll A. Deering*.

"It's a wild horse," she said. "Probably one of the mustangs."

"What mustangs?" Bailey asked.

"Usually, they're not this far south," Sydney told her, "and they don't typically come near people. They're wild horses—they don't belong to anyone. They wander as free

15

as any other wild animal around here. I'm pretty used to seeing them. They've lived on the Outer Banks for at least four hundred years, so people who live here don't pay much attention to them. They're another mystery of the Outer Banks. No one knows for sure how they got here."

"Oh great," said Bailey. "The sailors disappeared and nobody knows where they went. The wild horses showed up, but nobody knows how they got here. And this morning I saw a UFO.

"What kind of a place is this, Sydney? First you tell me a story about a ghost ship, and then a wild horse comes galloping by almost close enough to touch. You know, this sort of reminds me of *The Legend of Sleepy Hollow* where the headless horseman comes dashing out of nowhere."

"You never know," said Sydney. "We might have a headless horseman roaming around here, too. The Outer Banks is loaded with folklore about all kinds of stuff. It's even known for pirates like Captain Kidd, Calico Jack, and Blackbeard. They all walked along this beach once upon a time. Who knows, maybe they still do."

"Do you believe in ghosts?" Bailey asked.

Before Sydney could answer, a small ghost crab popped out of the sand and skittered toward the girls. It stopped briefly and looked at them through two black eyes set atop its head like periscopes sticking up from a submarine.

"Maybe," said Sydney, "and maybe not."

CHAPTER 2

The Disappearing Captain

The girls left the beach and walked to Corolla Village and the Currituck Beach Lighthouse. It was one of Sydney's favorite places, and she wanted to show it to Bailey. Something was wonderfully mysterious about the way the lighthouse rose from the trees and almost touched the sky. Its weathered red bricks sat tightly atop each other, forming rows around and around. They stopped at an iron-framed lookout. The lookout encircled the lantern house, the highest part of the tower. There, inside a giant, glass dome, was the powerful beacon of light that swept across ocean and sound.

Not far from the tower, nestled in a grove of trees, was a small lightkeeper's house. It had a steep red roof and white paint. The place was a gift shop where tourists could buy everything from tee shirts to figurines. Its wide front porch was empty but for a pair of old, wooden rocking chairs that often rocked alone in the wind.

Bailey and Sydney sat in the chairs looking up at the tower. Bailey nervously sipped the root beer that she'd bought at a little post office and convenience store nearby.

"You have to at least try," Sydney said.

"But I'm afraid of heights," Bailey answered. "You know that, Syd. In fact, if I could have, I would have walked here from Peoria instead of taking a plane." She swirled the root beer around in its plastic bottle.

"But you got on the airplane, and you got here in one piece," Sydney pointed out. "The next step is to climb to the top of the lighthouse."

Bailey glanced toward a short line of tourists waiting at the entrance. "How tall is it, anyway?"

"Not that tall," Sydney answered. She wrapped a napkin around the bottom of her ice-cream cone and licked the melting vanilla custard as it dribbled down the sides.

"How tall?" Bailey asked again.

"What difference does it make?" said Sydney.

"How tall!" Bailey demanded.

"I think two hundred fourteen steps to the top!"

"That's a lot."

"The Statue of Liberty has three hundred fifty-four steps," Sydney added. "You're always saying you want to go to New York and climb the Statue of Liberty. Think of this as your training. Once you've climbed the lighthouse, Lady Liberty will be a piece of cake."

"I dunno." Bailey sighed.

"And what about the Eiffel Tower?" Sydney went on. "You want to go to Paris and climb the Eiffel Tower. You told me that. And the Eiffel Tower is a whole lot scarier than the Currituck Beach Lighthouse."

"I guess so," Bailey agreed.

By now, Sydney had finished eating her custard and chomped on the cone. "Come on, Bailey," she said. "If you don't face your fears, you'll never climb the Statue of Liberty, or the Eiffel Tower either."

"I suppose you're right," Bailey said. She gulped down the rest of her root beer, got up, and tossed the empty bottle into a trash can. "Let's go."

"Go where?" Sydney answered.

"Let's climb to the top of the lighthouse before I chicken out."

The girls followed a curving brick path to the lighthouse entrance. A small, blue sign sat in front of the six concrete steps that led to the front door. It said: Please Wait Here to Climb. A family with three boys, all of them younger than Bailey and Sydney, stood waiting in line. The oldest one shoved his little brother and knocked him to the ground.

"Trevor!" his mother shouted. "Why did you push your brother?"

"He called me a name," Trevor said.

"I did not!" said the little brother getting up and standing next to his mom. "I want to go home."

"Behave!" said the dad.

Just then a gray-haired gentleman came from behind

the lighthouse. He walked toward the family, looking as if he'd stepped off a page in a history book. He wore a blue captain's cap, and his face was framed with a neat, gray beard. Although the weather was hot, he wore an old-fashioned blue wool officer's coat with shiny brass buttons and a nametag that read CAPTAIN SWAIN.

As Sydney and Bailey watched, the captain stopped in front of the boys. He opened his left fist and showed them four silver coins. "Spanish doubloons," he announced.

The boys gathered to see the treasure in the captain's hand. "Is this your first trip to the Outer Banks?" the captain asked.

"Yeah." The boys answered in unison.

"Then you don't know about the pirates," said the captain.

"What pirates?" Trevor asked. He grabbed Captain Swain's hand and pulled it closer to get a better look at the coins.

The old man smiled and looked Trevor straight in the eyes. "Blackbeard," he whispered.

Trevor stepped back.

"Blackbeard the pirate used to hide out on this very land," the captain said mysteriously. "He and his crew attacked ships at sea, robbed them, and brought their treasures back here to the Outer Banks. And these coins, my little friends, are some of the treasure that Blackbeard stole."

The boys' eyes grew big. They were so busy studying the doubloons that they didn't even notice when a group of visitors left the lighthouse.

"You're up next," Captain Swain told the family. "And when you get to the top, look out in the ocean as far as you can see. Maybe you'll spy Blackbeard's ship."

"Blackbeard doesn't exist," the older boy said. "He died a long time ago, and your coins are probably fakes."

"Trevor!" his mother scolded.

"Now, would I tell a tale?" said the captain. "Sure Blackbeard's dead, but some say his ghost haunts the sea while he and his crew sail on their ghost ship. You know about the ghost ships, don't you?"

The boys shook their heads.

"Then visit the museum down in Hatteras," the captain replied. "Graveyard of the Atlantic, it's called. They'll tell you all about Blackbeard and the ghost ships. You'll find a brochure inside." He pointed to the front door. Then, as the family disappeared into the entrance, Captain Swain turned to the girls. "Aren't you going with your family?" he asked.

"Oh, we're not with them," Sydney replied. "We're next in line."

The captain looked surprised. "How old are you young ladies?"

"Thirteen," said Sydney. She noticed the captain's sparkling, blue eyes.

"I'm nine," Bailey announced.

21

"Oh dear," said the captain. "Young people thirteen and under have to be accompanied by an adult. I'm afraid you won't be able to climb the lighthouse."

Bailey breathed a sigh of relief.

"But I'm *from* here!" Sydney protested. "Well, I'm not actually from here, but my grandparents have a beach house in Corolla Light. I visit them every year."

"Ah, the resort community," said the captain. He shook his head sadly. "I rarely get there. It's too crowded, and there's far too much traffic is on the highway. This is the *real* Corolla, you know. This tiny village was here long before Corolla Light or any of the other subdivisions."

"I know," said Sydney, "but can't we please climb the lighthouse? My friend Bailey is trying to overcome her fear of heights."

The captain winked at Bailey. "So, you're afraid of heights, are you? Well, we need to do something about that. The view from the top is outstanding. On one side there's the Atlantic Ocean, on the other side Currituck Sound."

Bailey's heart sank. She didn't really want to climb to the top of the lighthouse no matter how beautiful the view.

Captain Swain scratched his beard.

"I'll tell you what," he said. "I'll take you to the top. And, Bailey, you'll be fine. There's nothing to be afraid of. Nothing at all." He looked up at the tower, and Sydney noticed his mouth curl into a wistful smile.

Suddenly, the front door burst open. Trevor's little

brother scuttled out with his father close behind. "I am *not* being difficult," the boy shouted. "I don't want to climb those curvy steps. They're scary!"

His mother and brothers came out, too.

"Chicken!" Trevor taunted. He stood with his hands on his hips. "I wanted to go to the top, and now you've wrecked everything!"

"Let's go," said Trevor's dad. "I've had enough of this."

The mother grabbed the smallest boy's hand, and the family rushed to the parking lot.

"When justice is done, it brings joy to the righteous but terror to evildoers," said Captain Swain.

"What?" Sydney asked.

"Nothing," replied the captain. "Just God and me talking out loud. Looks like it's our turn to climb."

When they went inside, Bailey noticed how cool and stuffy the lighthouse felt. An ancient, brick wall circled them, and the narrow space smelled old. Sunlight streamed through several tall, narrow windows up high. In the center was a green, spiral staircase that reminded Bailey of a loosely coiled snake. Its metal stairs went up and up. When Bailey looked to where they led, she felt dizzy. She hesitated, afraid to take the first step.

Captain Swain seemed to know how she felt. " 'I can do all things through Him who strengthens me,' " he said.

Sydney gave him a quizzical look.

"Just God and me talking again," the captain announced.

23

Sydney knew that Bible verse from camp. It had given her courage when she was afraid.

"I want you to go first, Bailey," said the captain. "Your friend here—what's your name?" he asked, turning to Sydney.

"Sydney Lincoln," Sydney replied.

"Sydney Lincoln and I will be right behind you. We'll take very good care of you all the way. There's nothing to worry about. Absolutely nothing. I climbed these stairs a lot—back in the day."

The captain's voice echoed inside the tower. It seemed to drift all the way to the top and then disappear.

"I'll watch every step you take," Sydney told her. "You'll be fine. I promise."

Tentatively, Bailey put her right foot on the bottom step. She looked down to make sure that her shoes were tied. She didn't need to trip over any loose laces. Then she breathed deeply and whispered, " 'I can do all things through Him who strengthens me.' "

She put her left foot on the first step, and then Bailey Chang was on her way. She was ready to conquer her fear of heights and tackle all 214 steps. "One. Two. Three. Four." She counted each step unwaveringly, bravely marching upward. But then, she made the mistake of looking down. The stairs weren't solid. They had holes, like Swiss cheese, and when Bailey looked down at the fifty or so stairs she'd already climbed, she felt sick to her stomach. She stopped and Sydney almost tripped over her.

"Bailey! What?" Sydney wondered.

"I can't," Bailey whispered. "I'm afraid."

"Just move!" said Sydney. "This staircase is only wide enough for one person, and right now you've got us stuck here."

Bailey gripped the railings with both hands. Her feet wouldn't move. She was afraid to look up and afraid to look down. Her mind drifted to a strange place where she imagined she was the main character in a ghost story. She was stuck forever on that one step, an eerie mist that visitors sensed as they climbed to the top. Bailey Chang, Ghost of the Currituck Beach Lighthouse.

"Bailey." The captain's calm voice startled her. She grasped the railings even tighter. "I'm right here with you," he said. "I won't let anything happen to you. We're on our way now. You can do it. Just keep telling yourself that."

Bailey's heart slammed in her chest. Her mouth felt like sandpaper. She couldn't speak.

"Just one step, Bailey," said the captain. "Take one more step."

Bailey's feet moved up to the next step, whether she wanted them to or not.

"That's good," said the captain. "Now, one more."

Bailey felt Sydney close behind her. She decided if she fell backward onto her friend, and Sydney fell, too, the captain was strong enough to catch them both. So Bailey took the next step, and the next, and she kept going.

Whenever she got to a landing and one of the tall, narrow windows, Bailey avoided looking out. She wouldn't look down or up either. She just concentrated on one step at a time.

" 'I can do all things through Him who strengthens me,' " she murmured.

As she climbed the last steps, Bailey noticed a small landing and an old wooden door that stood wide open. She couldn't see where it led, but from where she stood Bailey caught a glimpse of blue sky and puffy, white clouds on the other side of it. She took the last step to the top and then turned away refusing to look beyond the door.

"You did it!" Sydney exclaimed. She stepped onto the landing and hugged her friend, but Bailey stood frozen.

"I'm not going out there," Bailey said. "I don't even want to see."

The captain stood between Bailey and the door. "It's your decision," he said. "But someday you might regret that you didn't. You might be sorry that fear got in your way."

Bailey swallowed hard.

"Come on, Bailey," Sydney coaxed. "Do you want to be an old lady telling your grandkids how scared you were? What kind of an example will that set?"

Bailey turned around. Beyond the captain's broad shoulders, she saw nothing but sky and clouds. Then, slowly, Captain Swain stepped aside. Bailey suddenly saw the tops of trees and in the distance, the Atlantic Ocean.

She felt like she was back in the airplane flying over North Carolina. But this time, if she chose to, she could step outside onto a narrow, open platform that was rimmed by a thick, iron railing.

The captain stepped outside. "I won't let anything happen to you," he said. "Sydney Lincoln, would you like to join me out here?"

Sydney's heart did a little flutter. She would never admit that she was scared, too. She had never climbed to the top of the lighthouse, and it was higher than she had imagined. Still, she wouldn't make Bailey more afraid than she already was.

Bravely, Sydney stepped through the door. She leaned against the captain and felt his strong arm holding her steady.

"It's not so bad, Bailey," she said, holding onto the railing. "Come on, we'll help you."

The captain held out his hand.

The image of herself as an old woman flashed through Bailey's mind. She heard herself say, "When I was little, I *almost* went out that door."

Bailey took the captain's hand, and then nothing stood between her and the world but the black, iron railing. Her stomach churned, but she inched along the lookout with her friends. They rounded the bend. Now, instead of seeing the ocean, they could see the sound—the strip of water between the Outer Banks' island and the shore of North Carolina.

"I knew you could do it, Bailey," said Sydney. "I watched you all the way, and you were really brave. I'm glad I convinced you to do it."

Bailey grabbed Sydney's arm. "Syd," she said. "Where'd the captain go? He was right behind me."

Captain Swain was gone! Just as if he had vanished into thin air!

A Mysterious Mug

"That's odd," said Sydney. "Where is he?"

A strong wind swept across the lighthouse. Sydney noticed Bailey's fingers gripping the railing. She grabbed Bailey's hand, and they carefully walked back to the door. When they got there, a lady whose name tag read MEGHAN was waiting.

"I was wondering if anyone was up here," she said. "I'm closing the lighthouse now. Storms are coming, and it's not safe up here when there's lightning."

The woman led the girls down the curving staircase. It was scarier going down than up because Sydney and Bailey had no choice but to look at their feet and imagine how far they'd fall if they tripped.

To keep her mind off it, Bailey began to talk—she tended to talk a lot whenever she got nervous. "So, do you like working in a lighthouse?" she asked.

"It's fascinating!" Meghan answered. "It's fascinating to go up to the top and see how the ocean changes every day."

"I live like two-and-a-half hours from Lake Michigan,"

Bailey told her. "And we go there in the summer to the beach and I think the lake looks a lot like the ocean, only it's not as big, and we have perch and trout instead of sharks and jellyfish."

She gulped a breath and went on. "Lake Michigan has fresh water and, of course, the ocean has salt water. This is the first time I've climbed a lighthouse. I'm afraid of heights, you know, but I climbed to the top—"

Sydney interrupted her. "Did you see Captain Swain come down the stairs?"

"Captain Swain? No," said Meghan. "Why?"

"He took us up to the lookout but disappeared. We didn't see him leave. We were wondering where he went." They were almost to the bottom of the stairs now, and Sydney sighed with relief.

"When was this?" the woman asked.

"Just a few minutes ago," said Sydney.

"I didn't see him come downstairs," Meghan replied as they reached the main floor. "As far as that goes, I didn't see him go up either. I must not have been paying attention."

"You weren't here," said Sydney. "When we came in, no one was around."

"That's odd," said Meghan. "I've been here for the past hour or so. I don't know how you got by without me seeing you, unless I was in my office. Did you say this was your first lighthouse visit?"

"It is," Bailey answered. "I'm visiting from Peoria. That's in Illinois."

"You know what?" said the lady. "I have something for you." She went to a desk in a little room nearby and picked up two small cardboard folders. "These are lighthouse passports," she said. She gave one to each of the girls. "You can visit lighthouses all over America and get stickers to put in your passport book. There's already a sticker from this lighthouse inside."

"Wow!" said Bailey. "I'm going to visit every lighthouse and collect all the stickers."

"If you do that, come back here and show me your passport. I'll buy you a cheeseburger," said Meghan.

"It might take me awhile to get them all," Bailey responded.

"Like, years!" Sydney added.

The woman smiled. "I imagine I'll be here."

After the girls left the lighthouse, Sydney pointed at two girls on the other side of Schoolhouse Lane. They were eating ice cream by the Corolla Village Bar-B-Q. "Come on," she told Bailey. "I want you to meet my friends." She led Bailey to a picnic table where the girls were sitting outside the restaurant. "Hi, Carolyn. Hi, Marilyn," said Sydney.

"Hi, Sydney!" the twins answered in unison. The Kessler twins often spoke in unison, Sydney had noticed. They were so much alike that Sydney still had trouble telling them apart, and she had known them for six years. The Kessler family owned a house near Sydney's grandparents' place. She knew they lived there year-round since Mr.

Kessler ran a company that made recreational water vehicles and racing boats.

"What are you guys doing here?" Sydney asked.

"Hanging out," they answered together.

"This is my friend, Bailey Chang," said Sydney.

"I thought so!" said Marilyn.

"I thought so, too," Carolyn echoed. "You're one of the Camp Club Girls. Sydney talks about you guys all the time."

Bailey slid into the bench at the picnic table. "Nice to meet you," she said. "We just finished climbing the lighthouse."

"You did!" the girls exclaimed.

"I've lived here since I was five, and I've never climbed it," said Marilyn.

"I haven't either," said Carolyn.

They both looked at Sydney as she slid into the bench next to Bailey. "Okay, I confess. I hadn't either," she said.

Bailey couldn't believe her ears. "What do you mean, you hadn't either? You acted like you'd climbed it a million times."

"I've always wanted to climb it," Sydney told her. "Would you have gone if I'd acted scared?"

Bailey thought for a second. "Well, no," she conceded. "But I wish I had known."

Two odd-looking bikes were propped against the picnic table. Each had two seats, two sets of handlebars, and two sets of pedals. "Are those your bikes?" Bailey asked the twins.

"They're tandems," said Carolyn.

Marilyn nodded in agreement. "Bicycles built for two." She took a lick of the chocolate ice cream that was melting in her cone.

"How come you *each* have one?" Bailey wondered. "Can't you both just ride on *one*?"

"One of them belongs to our brothers," said Carolyn. "The other one is ours."

"We just dropped them off at a friend's house on the Sound," said Marilyn. "They're spending the night there."

"And we're taking their bike home," Carolyn added. She popped the last bit of ice-cream cone into her mouth and Marilyn did the same with hers. "You can ride back with us, if you want to," she said. "We have our brothers' helmets you can wear."

Bailey looked at Sydney hoping she would agree.

"Okay," Sydney answered. "We probably should get home soon anyway. Gramps said Nate Wright might try to take a cluster balloon flight off the beach this afternoon. That'll be cool to watch."

"Who's going to do what?" Bailey asked. She looked at her reflection in the side-view mirror of one of the tandem bikes and smoothed her jet-black hair.

"Nate Wright is going to do a cluster balloon flight," said Sydney. "He ties a bunch of extra large helium party balloons to a chair contraption and sails up into the sky. Then he releases the balloons gradually to come back down."

"Why would he want to do that?" Bailey asked.

Carolyn climbed onto the front seat of one of the tandems and put on her helmet. "Mr. Wright's an inventor," she said, pointing for Bailey to get on the back seat.

"Well, sort of," said Marilyn, picking up the other bike and climbing onto the front seat. "He's kind of strange. He's always trying to invent weird ways to get around. Lately he's been experimenting with cluster ballooning."

"Mr. Wright's a distant relative of the Wright brothers," Carolyn explained. "Usually, people cluster balloon in the early morning when there's no breeze, but today, he's doing it in the afternoon."

"We saw his son on the beach this morning," Sydney said. "What's his name? Drake?"

"Yes, that's Drake Wright, Nate Wright's son," Marilyn said. "He's a beachcomber."

"They call him Digger," said Carolyn.

"He picks up junk along the beach and digs stuff out of the sand. Then he sells it to people who sell it in their shops or use it for crafts. Driftwood and glass floats and old fishing nets and stuff," Marilyn added. "And he hardly ever talks."

Carolyn gave her bike a shove with one foot and then started to pedal. Bailey held tight to the handlebars. She didn't know what to do when the pedals under her feet began to spin.

"Don't try to steer!" Sydney told her. "Just keep your feet

on the pedals and help Carolyn push."

Soon the girls were riding down Schoolhouse Lane heading for Corolla Light. They were almost to Highway 12—the two-lane road that was the main road for the Outer Banks—when Sydney's cell phone rang.

"Can we stop for a second?" she asked Marilyn. The twins steered their bikes to the side of the road. Sydney pulled her cell phone out of the pocket of her shorts. She flipped it open. "Hello?"

"Sydney," said a concerned voice that Sydney recognized as her grandfather. "Where are you?"

"We're biking home with the Kessler twins," Sydney answered. "We should be there in about ten minutes."

"Come straight home, and don't stop anywhere," said her grandfather. "A bad storm is coming, and I don't want you girls out in it."

"Okay, Gramps," said Sydney. "We're on our way." She folded the phone and slipped it back into her pocket. "There's a storm coming," she said. "Gramps wants us home."

"The sky does look kind of greenish and black over there," said Bailey, pointing to the right. "Do you guys have tornado warning sirens here?"

"I don't know," Sydney answered. "If they do, I've never heard one."

"Me neither," said Marilyn, steering her bike back onto the road.

35

"I haven't either. We don't usually have tornadoes here," said Carolyn, following her.

"They go off a lot in Peoria," Bailey said. "Sometimes, the sky looks ugly like this, and then we get a tornado warning."

Suddenly a bolt of lightning sliced through the black clouds.

Whoosh! The wind picked up. The girls pedaled as fast as they could. By the time they got to their street, big droplets of rain started to fall. Then the rain turned into a rushing waterfall that spilled onto the girls' helmets and soaked their clothing. The twins made a perfect turn into Sydney's driveway, and Sydney and Bailey hopped off the bikes. Then the Kesslers sped off toward home.

Sydney's grandparents stood on the upper deck of the beach house. "Hurry!" Gramps called to the girls. "Come on up here."

Sydney ran up the two flights of stairs with Bailey close behind.

Crash! At the sound of thunder, Bailey nearly tripped on the last step. She caught the railing and climbed up onto the covered deck.

Bailey, Sydney, and her grandparents stepped inside the sliding screen doors and watched the storm from the safety of the family room. The fierce purple cloud was right over their heads now. To the south, near the ocean's horizon, the sky was clear and the sun was shining. But north of the beach house, the scene was very different. A long, thin, white tail dropped from the cloud until it met the ocean. It turned brown as it sucked up water.

Bailey screamed. "Oh my goodness! Oh my goodness! It's a tornado!"

"If they're over the water, they're called waterspouts," Sydney's grandmother explained. "Then when they come to land, they're called tornadoes."

Bailey squeezed Sydney's arm.

"It's heading away from us," Sydney said as the cone swept out to sea. "Pretty soon it'll dwindle to nothing."

Gramps added, "We're safe here, but can you imagine being in a sailboat out in the ocean? A decent-sized waterspout could easily drop on one of those and smash a small boat to smithereens. In fact, that *did* happen. There are so many shipwrecks near the Outer Banks that folks have lost count."

"Maybe that's what happened to the sailors on the ghost ship," Sydney suggested. "They got sucked into a water spout."

Bailey watched the long, coiling twister disappear. Beyond it, in the distance, two more waterspouts formed as the ocean carried the storm away. The back edge of the dark cloud passed over the beach house now, and the rain turned to drizzle. Bailey wasn't afraid anymore. She thought the tumbling waves and the waterspouts were awesome.

37

"Lake Michigan has waterspouts, too," she said as the sun broke through the clouds. "I remember reading about them in current events, but I've never seen one. Very cool, although a bit scary."

"Look over there," said Sydney. The end of a rainbow was barely visible near the beach opposite of where the waterspout had been. Its colors gradually became bright, clear ribbons of red, orange, and yellow, blue, green, indigo, and violet.

"See?" said Sydney's grandmother. "God is sending us a message, just like He did to Noah on the ark. He's telling us we don't have to worry about the waterspout. It won't hurt us. A rainbow is God's way of saying, 'I promise.' "

"Let's go stand in the end of it!" Bailey was already out the door and running down the stairs toward the beach. Sydney followed, but by the time they got to where it looked like the rainbow ended, they realized it was out over the ocean.

"You can't touch it," Sydney explained when she caught up with Bailey. "Rainbows are sunlight bouncing off raindrops. I've chased them before, but you can't catch them. They move with the rain."

Bailey looked at her sand-caked feet. "Hey, look!" she said. "I'm wearing sand shoes."

She dropped to her knees and began scooping wet sand into a big pile. "Come on, Syd, let's make a sandcastle or something."

Sydney sat near her friend and helped form sand into a mound. "You know, don't you, that the tide will come in and wash it away."

Bailey patted the sand with both hands, sculpting it into a tower. "I don't care," she said. "Building it is the fun part."

"I see something we can use," said Sydney. A cylinder-shaped container was half-buried in the sand nearby. Sydney went to get it. "This'll work," she said. "We can put wet sand in here and mold it into turrets."

The container that Sydney found was a tall, insulated coffee mug. The top was screwed on so tight that she couldn't get it off. She tipped the mug, and water dribbled out of the tiny hole on top. She shook it, and the inside rattled.

"Something's in here," she said. Sydney shook the mug again, but nothing fell out. She shook it harder. Still nothing. Then she peeked into the hole.

"I can't see anything," she said. "This is kind of gross. We should wash it or something." She walked to the water's edge and swished the mug in the ocean. Then, once more, she looked inside. Nothing. She turned the mug upside down and shook it hard and fast.

A beam of light jiggled across the sand!

"Bailey? I think it's glowing!"

"Huh?" said Bailey, who hadn't been paying attention.

"It's glowing. The mug is glowing!" Sydney repeated. She turned the mug upright. A bright beam of light streamed out of the tiny opening. She put her eye to the opening, but the light was too bright to see what was inside.

Bailey put her hand a few inches above the tiny hole. A small circle of light reflected on the palm of her hand.

"Weird," she said. "What do you think this is?"

"Beats me," Sydney answered. "I've never seen a coffee mug that lights up."

"Me neither," Bailey replied. "Maybe it's not a coffee mug at all. Maybe we've stumbled onto something else."

"Like what?" Sydney asked, handing her the mug.

Bailey sat down and chewed her lip, a nervous habit that she vowed to break. "Like, maybe, some sort of secret weapon," she said. "Something the UFO left behind."

"If it were a secret weapon, we'd probably be dead by now," Sydney told her. "Your imagination is getting away from you again."

The girls sat for a few minutes pondering the odd gadget and then—

"Hey, the light went out!" Bailey exclaimed.

UFO!

The object was indeed strange. It seemed to light up only after Bailey or Sydney shook it for a while. Then, it cast an eerie glow for about five minutes and went dark. They brought it back to the beach house, and Sydney put it on a metal bookshelf in the guest room. She had the idea that they might try to dissect it later.

When the Camp Club Girls met in their chat room after supper, Sydney told them about the mug.

> Kate: *A coffee mug that glows from the inside? Why would you need it to light up inside?*
> Alexis: *Maybe it's so you can see how much coffee's left.*
> McKenzie: *But you have to shake it to make it light. That doesn't make sense, because if there's hot coffee, you'll get burned when it leaks out of the hole on top.*
> Elizabeth: *I think you can close the hole. My mom's coffee mug has a flippy thing you*

*turn to open and close the hole. Oh, and by
the way, the kind of mug you have is a
travel mug. Some of them aren't supposed
to be submerged in water. At least my
mom's can't.*

Sydney: *Maybe it got dropped in the ocean
and the salt water wrecked it or something,
and then it washed up on the beach.*

Bailey took the laptop from Sydney.

Bailey: *Hi, Bettyboo. Hi, everyone else.*
Elizabeth: *You know I don't like being called
Bettyboo.*
Bailey: *Just kidding, Beth. I have a theory
about the mug. It was half buried in the
sand. I don't think it washed up on the
shore. Someone put it there. I think it's
some kind of secret weapon.*

She bit her lip hard and waited for someone to reply.

Alexis: *Something like that happened in one
old alien movie I saw.*
McKenzie: *Why would you think it's a weapon?*
Bailey: *I don't know. It's too creepy to be
anything ordinary.*

She pushed the laptop back to Sydney and went to get the mug from the bookshelf. She grabbed the handle, but the mug wouldn't budge.

"Hey," she said. "It's stuck."

"What do you mean?" Sydney asked.

"It's glued to the bookshelf, Bozo," said Bailey. "I can't pick it up!"

"Oh for goodness' sake," said Sydney. She set the computer on the twin bed, where they had been cyber-chatting, and she went to help Bailey.

Sydney grasped the mug's handle. Bailey was right. It was stuck. She pulled hard. The mug let loose, almost catapulting her backward.

"See?" said Bailey. She examined the spot where the mug had been. "I don't see any glue or other sticky stuff."

Sydney moved closer to inspect the bare spot. All at once, the mug shot out of her hand and stuck itself to the shelf. "It's a magnet!" Sydney gasped. "Look at this." She yanked the mug away from the metal shelf and then let it fly back. "I didn't notice it when I put the mug here before."

"Way cool!" Bailey squealed.

Sydney hurried back to the laptop to tell the girls. When she looked at the screen, she found a string of messages.

> Alexis: *Syd? Bailey? Where are you?*
> McKenzie: *Hey, did you log off without saying good-bye?*

Kate: *Where did everybody go?*

Sydney: *Sorry. Bailey went to get the mug, and we found out it's a magnet! It was stuck to my metal bookshelf.*

Kate: *DANGER! DANGER! Do not—I repeat—DO NOT put that mug anywhere near the computer.*

Bailey was just about to plop down on the bed next to Sydney with the mug in her hand. "No!" Sydney yelled. She shoved Bailey off the bed and onto the floor.

"Hey!" Bailey protested. She sat there looking startled. "What did you do that for?"

"I'm sorry," said Sydney. "Kate just wrote that the mug is very dangerous—"

Bailey shuddered and flung the coffee mug over her shoulder. It landed somewhere across the room. "What's the matter with it?" she asked nervously.

"You didn't let me finish," said Sydney. "It's dangerous to put it near the computer."

Sydney told the girls what had just happened.

Alexis: *Well, at least now you know that it's not a bomb. The way you two are messing with it, it would have gone off by now.*

Bailey joined Sydney on the bed. She read what Alex had just written.

Bailey: *Not funny. Why is it dangerous to put
a coffee mug next to a laptop?*

Kate: *I read a magnet will kill the pixels on
your computer screen, so it's best to keep
the mug away from it. Can you take a
video with your cell phone?*

Sydney: *No, but I can with my digital
camera.*

Kate: *Good. Stand away from the computer
and shoot a video to show us what you do
to make it light up.*

Sydney retrieved the mug from a corner of the room.

"You hold it," said Bailey. "I don't want to touch it."

"It won't bite you," Sydney answered. She got her digital camera out of her dresser drawer.

Bailey took the pink camera out of Sydney's hand and turned it on. She switched the button to VIDEO MODE. "All set," she said. "Ready?" Bailey pushed another button and started recording. "The case of the mysterious cup. Take One!"

Sydney held the mug and shook it hard, but nothing happened.

"It stopped recording," said Bailey. "The LCD says, 'OUT OF MEMORY.' "

"My camera only takes a forty-five-second video," Sydney answered. "Don't start recording as soon as I shake it."

Bailey deleted the first video, and the girls tried again. Sydney shook the mug hard and fast, but again, the time ran out before anything happened.

Sydney sighed. "Hang on a minute. I'll shake the mug to see how long it takes to light up." Sydney shook the mug hard, but it wouldn't light. "Bailey, I think you broke it."

"I did not!" Bailey defended herself.

Sydney tried again, but the mug stayed dark.

By the time they returned to the computer, Kate had an idea.

> Kate: *You know, that thing reminded me of my shake flashlight, so while you were away I went on the Internet and looked up how it works.*
>
> McKenzie: *What's a shake flashlight?*
>
> Kate: *Don't you have them in Montana? It looks like a regular flashlight, but it doesn't work on batteries. It has a strong magnet inside. When you shake it, the magnet passes up and down through a coil. That causes the capacitor to charge and the flashlight lights!*
>
> Alexis: *Now you have a perfectly reasonable explanation.*
>
> Bailey: *But there's nothing reasonable about a glowing coffee cup.*

"Mug," Sydney corrected her. It bugged her when people misused words.

> Bailey: *In fact, a lot of unreasonable stuff has gone on since I got here last night.*
> McKenzie: *Like what?*
> Bailey: *I saw strange lights over the water that looked like a UFO. Today I stepped on a bone on the beach and Syd said it might have come from a dead sailor. A lot of them have disappeared around here. Like when a ghost ship washed up on the beach down the coast. The sailors vanished into thin air. Then, today we climbed a lighthouse with an old sea captain but he disappeared. maybe he was a ghost, too.*
> Elizabeth: *Bailey, calm down. There are no ghosts!*

Bailey chewed on her lip as her fingers flew across the keyboard.

> Bailey: *There are, too! There's the Holy Ghost. We learned about Him at camp, and I heard my pastor talk about Him.*
> Elizabeth: *The Holy Ghost is a part of the*

47

Trinity of God. Sure, He's a spirit, and you can't see Him, but He's not out to get you. There are no such things as ghosts.

Bailey said no more. Elizabeth was the oldest of the Camp Club Girls, and she seemed to know everything about God. Sometimes, Bailey felt like such a kid when she was around her.

Kate: *So what are you going to do with it?*
Sydney: *I don't know. Throw it in the trash, I guess.*
Kate: *Gotta go. Biscuit just made a mess, and I have to clean it.*

It was getting late, and the rest of the girls decided to sign off, too.

Bailey and Sydney's guest room in the beach house was on the second floor. It had two twin beds with matching striped bedspreads and big, fluffy pillows. A white wicker nightstand separated the beds, and it held an alarm clock and a table lamp made out of seashells. The room was painted a soft blue, and instead of one wall, two big sliding glass doors led to a private covered deck that overlooked the ocean. Gramps had said that Bailey and Sydney could sleep out there if they wanted to. It would be like camping, only instead of sleeping in a cabin near Discovery Lake, they would sleep under the stars near the beach. The girls got their sleeping bags and went outside.

"Hey, what's going on down there?" asked Bailey. She leaned over the deck railing to get a better look. Below, children ran around on the beach with plastic buckets and flashlights.

"Ghost crab hunting," said Sydney as she settled into a hammock on one end of the deck.

"Ghost crabs? You mean that ugly thing that we saw on the beach this morning?"

"They're not ugly," Sydney said. "I think they're kind of cute."

"They look like monster white spiders," said Bailey. "Why is everyone trying to catch them?"

Sydney rolled on her side and gazed at the ocean. "Because they're fun to chase," she said. "They pop in and out of their holes so fast you never know when you'll find one. Little kids especially like looking for them."

She paused and watched the moonlight dance across the waves. "They're hard to catch, because they blend in with the sand. Sometimes, if you stay real still and wait, it's like the sand comes alive around your feet. The ghost crabs come up out of their holes all around you, and then they start scurrying sideways and if you move—even one tiny little bit—*they bite your toes*!" Sydney made a quick grab at Bailey's foot.

Bailey jumped. "Ooo! Don't scare me like that," she said.

"I've heard enough ghost stories for one day."

Sydney rolled onto her back and gazed up at the stars. "Like Elizabeth said, Bailey, there's no such things as ghosts."

"Then how do you explain the captain disappearing?" asked Bailey.

"I don't know where the captain went," Sydney said, "but I don't think he was a ghost that just floated off the top of the lighthouse."

Down below, on the beach, children giggled and screamed with delight as they tried to put crabs into plastic buckets.

"Be careful!" a man's called in the darkness. "They pinch!"

"Hey, look up there. It's the big dipper," Sydney said, changing the subject. She pointed out the constellation to Bailey, and the girls settled down to watch the stars, Sydney in the hammock and Bailey on a mattress on the deck. Soon they were sound asleep.

Bailey had a nightmare. She dreamed that she was climbing the stairs in the lighthouse, and they disappeared beneath her. There was no way down and no way out.

She awoke with a start. The full moon was high in the sky, casting a glow on the water. The beach was deserted, and Bailey had no idea what time it was. She stood and looked out at the sea.

The waves washing up on the beach glowed an eerie blue green, and she saw what looked like glowing ghost crabs skittering across the sand.

"Sydney!" she whispered. "Wake up!"

Sydney groaned and rubbed her eyes. "What's the matter?"

"Get up!" Bailey demanded. "The ocean is glowing and so are the crabs."

"Huh?" asked Sydney. She sat up wearily and looked at the beach. "It's just bioluminescence."

"Buy a luma what sense?"

"Bioluminescence," Sydney repeated. "It's a phenomenon caused by phosphorous in the water. On moonlit nights, it makes the waves glow."

"And crabs, too?" Bailey wondered.

"I suppose," said Sydney. "It's nothing to worry about. Go back to sleep." Sydney rolled over, and in no time at all, Bailey heard her breathing heavily.

She felt lonely on the deck with Sydney sleeping. At night, the ocean didn't seem at all like Lake Michigan. The Atlantic was huge, and it held sharks and stingrays, and who knows what else. And scorpions and snakes might be nearby. If they were on the beach, they could find their way up to the deck where the girls slept.

Although it was muggy outside, Bailey climbed into her sleeping bag and zipped it up tight. She sat on the deck with her back against the wall, fighting sleep. She worried that if she slept she might have another nightmare.

Dawn was peeking over the ocean when Bailey lifted her head. She had dozed off sitting up and now her back ached. The moonlight had faded, and the ocean was like a black, gaping hole. She thought she heard something on the beach. It was a soft whirring sound, kind of like the blade of a helicopter spinning. It stopped. Then she heard nothing but the waves lapping up on the sand.

Bailey climbed out of her sleeping bag and stood by the railing. Something caught her eye. There, not far offshore, was some sort of flying thing. Bailey could barely make out its shape, but it was the size of a car and covered with blinking, multicolored lights. It moved slowly, hovering above the water.

"Sydney! Wake up!" Bailey commanded. She ran to the hammock and shook her friend awake.

"What!" Sydney exclaimed.

"Get up!" said Bailey. "The UFO is out there!"

Sydney sat up and looked toward the ocean. "Bailey, nothing is there. That story I told you about people seeing things at night? It's just a story. I don't believe there's anything to it."

When Bailey looked toward where the lights had been, she saw they were gone. "Oh, Syd," she gasped. "You have to believe me. Something dreadful is out there."

"I believe you," Sydney said halfheartedly. "Now, forget it, and go back to sleep."

"I won't!" said Bailey. "Look!"

Mysteries on the Beach

"Whoa! What on earth is that?" Sydney exclaimed.

The object was making small, tight circles above the water and darting to and fro. It's blinking lights alternated from red to multicolored, and it didn't make a sound that the girls could hear from their balcony.

"It's not on earth," Bailey answered, "And it's not *from* earth either. It's a UFO! I told you so. I'll go get your grandparents." Bailey started for the sliding glass doors.

"Not yet," said Sydney. "It's probably nothing. Let's go check it out."

She climbed out of the hammock and put on her sandals.

"Are you crazy?" Bailey shrieked.

"Sshhhh!" Sydney told her. "You'll wake everybody."

"We are *not* going to check it out," Bailey whispered. "What if the aliens on it abduct us and take us to their planet? No way, Syd!"

But Sydney was already hurrying down the stairs to the beach.

"Don't leave me alone," Bailey begged.

"Then come on," her friend said.

The UFO was just offshore now. The blinking lights faded to black, and the object disappeared into the darkness. Soon a strange whirring came from the water's edge. It turned into a soft *flop flop flop*, sounding like a flat tire on asphalt. Whatever it was had landed on the beach. And it was moving!

Sydney walked toward the noise, but she couldn't see a thing.

The noise stopped.

Bailey had Sydney by the arm now and held her back from going even closer.

Whoof!

A strong puff of hot air hit the girls in the face. Something whizzed past them only a few yards away.

"A wild horse!" Bailey gasped.

"That was no horse," Sydney said.

"Are you sure?" asked Bailey. She loosened her grip.

"I'm sure," said Sydney. "It was going so fast that it's probably to the sound by now."

Sydney decided to run home to get a flashlight. Bailey insisted on coming along. In only moments, the girls returned to the place where whatever it was had rushed past them. Sydney focused the light onto the sand at the water's edge.

"Oh my," she said, "look at that!"

Along the water was a line of strange footprints in the wet sand.

Or were they footprints?

The prints were like big, oval waffles. Their pattern of lines and squares looked like someone had gone along slapping the sand with a tennis racket. The prints came out of the sea and stretched only across the wet sand at the ocean's edge. When they reached the dry part of the sand, they disappeared.

"Bigfoot!" said Bailey. "You know, that gigandamundo monster that leaves his footprints but is hardly ever seen!"

"There's no such thing as Bigfoot," Sydney said. She crouched down to get a better look.

"And until a few minutes ago, you didn't believe UFOs existed," said Bailey.

She had a point. Sydney had no idea what they had just witnessed. She had no explanation for the strange thing that hovered over the water or for the way that it had rushed past them on the beach without a sound.

As she looked over the ocean, Sydney saw the sun beginning to rise. It painted the sky a beautiful salmon orange and sent diamonds of light dancing across the lavender-colored sea.

"Bailey, go get the camera," Sydney said. "We have to get a picture of these prints before they wash away."

Bailey ran to the beach house. She quickly returned to where Sydney waited. By the time she got there, the water was already lapping at the prints.

Sydney snapped a half dozen shots until the prints had almost disappeared.

"Looking for ghost crabs, Sydney Lincoln?"

A man's deep voice came from behind them.

"Captain Swain!" Bailey exclaimed. "What are you doing here?"

The captain stood in front of them dressed in a crisp blue jogging suit. Sydney noticed it had a coastguard emblem on one sleeve. He had a dog with long black fur, about the size of Kate's dog, Biscuit, by his side.

"McTavish and I are taking our morning walk," the captain replied. "And what brings you girls out so early on this fine, summer morning."

"We saw a UFO," Bailey answered. "And then we went to check it out, but it disappeared. Now there are Bigfoot prints in the sand."

Bailey didn't notice that Sydney was shooting her a look that said, *"Be quiet!"* By now, the footprints had been completely washed away.

" 'So we fix our eyes not on what is seen, but on what is unseen. For what is seen is temporary, but what is unseen is eternal,' " the captain said.

In the back of her mind, Sydney remembered reading those words in her Bible study class at camp, but she wasn't quite sure what they meant.

"Just God and me talking out loud," said the captain. He

bent and patted McTavish on the head. The dog wagged its tail, sending sand flying in all directions. "Go play, my boy," the captain said, and McTavish scampered along the water's edge leaving footprints trailing behind him.

"I thought you said you never come to Corolla Light," Sydney reminded him.

"I said I *rarely* come here," the captain corrected her. "I *never* come here in the daytime when things are busy unless I absolutely have to. Too many tourists! But often in the morning hours, I hear the ocean calling me."

Bailey still wasn't sure about Captain Swain. Something about him was different. He seemed not to fit in with the residents and tourists on the Outer Banks. She imagined him instead in the days of the ghost ships, hoisting the billowing sails, and standing at the ship's wheel. He seemed mysterious. From a different time in history.

She decided to come right out and ask, "Are you a—"

"Girls! Breakfast!" Sydney's grandmother stood on the upper deck of the beach house calling to them. "Come on, now."

"We have to go," Sydney said. She and Bailey ran back to the house.

"Who was that man?" Sydney's grandma asked. "And why were you girls on the beach so early?"

"We saw a UFO," Bailey announced. "And we went to check it out, but we didn't find anything but Bigfoot's footprints. And then Captain Swain showed up. I think he's a ghost because yesterday he disappeared into thin air." She looked down at the beach, but the captain was gone.

"See," she said. "He disappeared *again*!"

Sydney looked toward the beach and tried to come up with a logical explanation.

"Did you see where he went, Grandma?" she asked.

Sydney's grandmother looked north and south.

"No," she replied. "But I had my eyes on you and not on the beach. Bailey, UFOs and Bigfoot and ghosts don't exist. Those are all just stories." Her brown eyes twinkled as she smiled at Sydney's friend. "We're so happy to have you here, but we don't want you to be afraid of things that don't exist. We just want you to have fun."

Bailey still wasn't convinced. She had seen the UFO with her own eyes, and she had seen the footprints, too. And those footprints weren't from any animal or human.

"But those things do exist," she whispered to herself. "At least, I think so."

The girls hurried to their room to dress. Sydney quickly e-mailed the photos to the Camp Club Girls, telling them what had happened at the beach that morning. Then she and Bailey dashed to the kitchen table. Grandpa said the mealtime prayer:

"Loving Father, we thank You for this food,
And for all Your blessings to us.
Lord Jesus, come and be our guest,
And take Your place at this table.

Holy Spirit, as this food feeds our bodies,
So we pray You would nourish our souls. Amen."

"Is the Holy Spirit the same as the Holy Ghost?" Bailey asked as she chose a piece of cinnamon bread.

"He is," Gramps answered, scooping some scrambled eggs onto Bailey's plate.

"And He's truly a ghost?" Bailey wondered.

"He's a spirit, Bailey," Gramps answered. "Many things about God are a mystery and beyond what we humans can understand. The Holy Spirit is one of them. He's a part of God, but He isn't a ghost who haunts or hurts people. He's the Helper, the One who guides us through every day. Grandma says you've been seeing things since you got here."

Bailey shook some pepper onto her eggs. She didn't know what to say except that she had seen strange things, and they were real.

"You girls are good at solving mysteries," Sydney's grandfather went on. "I think you've discovered, by now, that when it comes to mysteries there's usually a logical explanation."

Sydney went to the refrigerator and got a slice of American cheese. She put it on top of her scrambled eggs and zapped her meal in the microwave.

"I think it's my fault," she said. "Yesterday, I told Bailey about the ghost ship. Since then, she's been thinking about ghosts." Sydney carried her eggs back to the table and stuck her fork into the gooey cheese.

"Ah, the ghost ship," Gramps said. "That's an unsolved mystery on the Outer Banks. Folks like to make up stories about it. Somewhere, though, there's the truth about what happened to those poor missing sailors. You can be sure there's a good explanation."

Gramps stirred cream into his coffee. "You know, I think tomorrow I'll take you girls to the Graveyard of the Atlantic Museum. Then you can learn all about the ghost ship and the other shipwrecks off the coast."

While the girls continued eating and talking about shipwrecks, someone knocked on the door and Sydney's grandmother went to answer it.

In a moment, the Kessler twins walked into the room, greeting the girls. Grandpa offered them some cinnamon bread, but they declined.

"Hey, Nate Wright is down at the beach near Tuna Street, and he's setting up his chair," Marilyn said.

"Digger is starting to blow up the helium balloons," Carolyn added. "And I thought Bailey might want to see."

"Can we?" Sydney asked her grandparents as she picked up her plate and Bailey's to carry to the dishwasher.

"Go ahead," Grandma said. "But when he takes off, you girls stay a safe distance away. I don't want you getting hurt." Grandma sipped her coffee. "Cluster ballooning is dangerous, even when it's done the ordinary way, but when

Nate does it, it's even more dangerous. He takes too many risks if you ask me and is even a bit crazy. And that son of his is an odd duck, too."

Grandma poured a little more creamer into her coffee. "Why, you wouldn't believe the junk that boy picks up on the beach. One day, I was near their house in the village, and you should have seen the junk piled up by their equipment shed!"

"One night, our dad had to go to the village, and he saw Mr. Wright and Digger welding stuff in their yard," Marilyn said. "The sparks lit up their place like fireworks on the Fourth of July. He said he heard that they get real busy at night moving stuff around in the dark—"

"And using hammers and power saws, too," Carolyn added.

Grandpa buttered a piece of bread for himself. "Nate says he's an inventor, but the only invention I've seen so far is that silly balloon chair. He thinks he can use that idea to someday create travel that's fast, clean, and inexpensive. Can you imagine all of us flying around in chairs tethered to party balloons?"

The girls laughed.

"Let's go," said Sydney. "Are we walking or taking our bikes?"

"Walking," said the twins.

The girls joined a small crowd that had gathered on the beach just off the sandy beach access lane. Nate Wright was checking the chair, adjusting the straps and making sure they were secured. The seat looked like it came from an airplane cockpit. It had lots of instruments and a big joystick.

"It'll never get off the ground," Bailey said. "It'll be too heavy with all that stuff on it."

"No, it won't," said Sydney. "You won't believe your eyes."

An old beat-up school bus was parked at the edge of the beach on the end of the access road. On its side was a hodgepodge of words:

LASERS

LEVITATING

ELEVATING

WRIGHT &

SON

ORIENTEERING

RACING

"What does it all mean?" Bailey asked.

"I guess it advertises things they're working on. I don't really know," said Sydney.

"Why don't we ask them?" said Bailey.

"Because they don't talk to anybody," Sydney replied. "The only time the Wrights say anything is if they think you're getting close enough to get hurt."

Drake Wright, Digger, was on the roof of the bus with a helium tank. One-by-one, he filled balloons with helium and fastened them to big hooks on top of the bus roof. Each hook held several dozen colorful balloons.

"What's he doing?" asked Bailey.

"He has to have a place to store the balloons until they get attached to the chair," said Marilyn. "So he ties them to the bus, because anything lighter than a bus would lift right off the ground."

"No way!" said Bailey. She took her cell phone out of her pocket and snapped a few pictures. "I'm going to send these to Kate right now," she said. "She'll love this!"

Once Digger had filled all of the balloons, he helped his dad slide the chair to the front of the school bus. Then they chained and locked it to the bumper. Mr. Wright sat down, strapped himself in, and put on a helmet, the kind the astronauts wear.

"Now what?" asked Bailey.

"Watch," said Carolyn.

"Watch," Marilyn echoed.

Methodically, Digger carried the balloons from the rooftop to his dad's chair, one bunch at a time. He attached them to special fasteners on the chair frame and the chair soon began to rise.

"Awesome!" Bailey gasped, snapping more pictures.

"You haven't seen anything yet," said Sydney.

When all of the balloons were in place, the chair

hovered near the hood of the school bus. It strained to break loose.

"Get back!" Digger yelled at the crowd.

Everyone took several steps backward.

Drake shook his dad's hand and released the chains. The chair shot up into the air like a rocket. It kept soaring up and over the water.

"Oh wow!" said Bailey.

Digger disappeared from sight.

"Where'd he go?" Bailey asked, snapping a few more pictures.

"He's probably gone to get the boat," said Carolyn.

"Mr. Wright can only go so high before the oxygen gets too thin," said Marilyn, "so he has to start popping balloons to slowly come down. When he splashes down in the ocean, Digger will be there to pick him up."

"But Digger has to go down the shore a bit to get the boat in the water," Carolyn explained to the girls. "There's no dock or boat ramp here, and you have to have a boat with some power to withstand the waves."

"He usually flies over the sound side of the Outer Banks," Marilyn said. "That's where most of the smaller boats and jet skis are because the water is calmer."

Bailey's cell phone rang. It was a text message from Kate: READ THE FIRST LETTERS OF EACH WORD ON THE BUS FROM BOTTOM TO TOP. THEY SPELL ROSWELL! K8

"Check it out," Bailey said handing the phone to

Sydney. "What's Roswell?"

Sydney read the message. "Roswell is a town in New Mexico famous for UFOs," she explained. "People think one crashed there years ago."

Pop! Pop-pop! Pop!

As a series of a loud bangs rang over the ocean the girls wondered about UFOs as they watched Nate Wright's chair fall slowly toward the sea.

CHAPTER 6

Aliens

Dear Syd and Bailey,
Kate e-mailed me about the Wrights
and the Roswell connection. How creepy! Do
you think that the Wrights are connected with
the UFO you saw this morning? I don't know
if you've seen the movie Close Encounters
of the Third Kind, *but in the movie people*
tried to make contact with a spaceship by
using a code—five musical notes, re-mi-do-
do-sol. I wonder if that flashlight thing you
found on the beach is some sort of signaling
device. Do you think the Wrights are trying to
communicate with aliens?

> *Be careful,*
> *Alex*

Alexis's e-mail, marked HIGHEST PRIORITY, was waiting
for Sydney and Bailey when they got back from the beach.

"Now do you believe me?" Bailey asked flopping on

her bed in the guest room. "Even Alex thinks we're being invaded by spaceships."

Sydney sat on her bed fidgeting with her cornrows. She was trying to find a practical explanation.

"I don't know what to believe," she answered. "I mean, Roswell is another unsolved mystery like the ghost ship. According to the story, a UFO crashed in Roswell, in the desert. A rancher found pieces of metal scattered all over his property. He called the authorities and even the army got involved. It was a very big deal back then. They roped off his land and didn't let anyone inside. At first the government said they found pieces of a flying saucer. Later they said that the pieces were from a weather balloon. No one knows for sure, but just like the ghost ship story, rumors have kept going around."

Bailey lay on her bed thinking. She was sure the UFO she saw was not a helicopter, boat, or other ordinary thing. If the Wrights were involved, it would make sense, because they were so different and secretive.

"Hey," said Bailey. "Maybe they're aliens!"

"Huh?" said Sydney.

"Mr. Wright and Digger," Bailey answered. "Maybe their spaceship crashed in the ocean, but they survived. That would explain Drake Digger picking up stuff along the shore. He's picking up pieces of the spaceship!"

Sydney sighed. "Oh, Bailey, your imagination is getting away from you again."

"No, it's not," said Bailey sitting up on the bed. "At night, when most people are asleep, the Wrights are trying to reconstruct their spaceship from the pieces Drake finds. That's why they're welding and stuff. And meanwhile they're trying to create an alternate vehicle that could go high enough to meet a rescue ship, or something. That's why they're experimenting with the cluster balloons. And that thing we found on the beach? Alex is right. It's a signaling device."

"Bailey!" said Sydney.

"And you know what else?" Bailey went on. "I think Captain Swain is one of them. He was on the beach this morning when the UFO was there. He saw the whole thing! *He* knows what that thing was hovering over the ocean, and he knows what scooted past us in the dark. He knows about those footprints, too!"

"Oh, Bailey, stop," said Sydney. "Yesterday, you thought the captain was a ghost." She got up from her bed and got the coffee mug from the bookshelf.

"I don't think he's a ghost anymore," said Bailey. "Now I think he's a space alien."

Sydney shook the coffee mug, but nothing happened. She shook it again. Still nothing. Then she tossed it into the wastebasket. It landed with a thud. "Enough of the alien stuff already!" she said. She slid open the glass doors to the deck and went outside.

Bailey screamed at the top of her lungs.

"What's the matter?" Sydney exclaimed, hurrying back inside.

Bailey was sitting on the bed, her knees pulled tight to her chest with her arms wrapped around them. She looked terrified.

"Bailey, what's wrong?" Sydney asked again.

Bailey pointed to the wastebasket. The inside of it was lit with an eerie, flashing light. Sydney looked more closely and saw that it was coming from the hole in the lid of the mug.

This was too weird. For the first time, Sydney believed no logical explanation existed for the mug, the UFO, or any of the other strange things that had been going on. She bent to take the mug out of the trash, but then she stopped.

Better to leave it alone, she thought.

"Count 'em, Syd. Count 'em," said Bailey.

"Count what?" Sydney asked.

"Count the flashes of light," Bailey answered. "One, two, three, four, five. . . One, two, three, four, five. . ."

The mug sent out five quick flashes of light. Then it stopped briefly and sent out five more.

"So?" said Sydney.

"So, remember what Alex said in her e-mail?" Bailey answered. "In the *Close Encounters* movie, the signal was five musical notes. One, two, three, four, five notes. One, two, three, four, five flashes of light. It's a code, Sydney."

Bailey's phone dinged. It was another message from

Kate. Bailey read aloud. "BAILEY, DO YOU KNOW ABOUT THE LAKE MICHIGAN TRIANGLE AND THE FOOTPRINTS? IF NOT, LOOK IT UP ONLINE. K8." There was a URL address.

"What's the Lake Michigan Triangle?" Sydney asked.

"Never heard of it," said Bailey. "Let's check it out."

Sydney typed the URL address into the browser window on her computer. An article from a Michigan newspaper appeared on the screen. She read, then explained.

"This says the Lake Michigan Triangle has a history similar to the Bermuda Triangle. The lines of an imaginary triangle run from Ludington, Michigan, down to Benton Harbor, Michigan, then across the lake to Manitowoc, Wisconsin, and back across the lake to Ludington."

"I know where Manitowoc is," Bailey said. "Our family rented a cottage near there one summer."

Sydney continued. "Ships have disappeared inside the triangle. This even says one of them is seen sailing on the lake from time to time, but then disappears."

"Another ghost ship!" said Bailey. "And that's not too far from where I live. Do you know what, Syd? I just remembered something."

"What?" Sydney asked.

"A couple of years ago, there was a report of a UFO over O'Hare International Airport, in Chicago. Pilots saw it, and some other people did, too. They said it was shaped like a saucer and spun around slowly, but didn't make any noise.

The air traffic controllers couldn't see it on the radar. Then, *zoom!* It shot straight up into the sky."

"For real?" asked Sydney.

"Really," Bailey answered. "It was in the *Chicago Tribune* and on the TV news, too. Nobody ever found out what it was."

"Check this out," said Sydney, reading the article. "There have also been reports of strange footprints on the beach near the points of the triangle."

Bailey gasped. "Footprints! Syd, maybe those footprints were like the ones we saw this morning. Alien footprints!"

Sydney logged off her browser. "You know, Bailey," she said, "maybe UFOs do exist."

Bailey got up the courage to walk to the wastebasket and peer inside. The flashing light had stopped. Once again, the thing looked like an ordinary travel mug. "So what do we do now?" she asked.

"We put the mug back where we found it," said Sydney. "Then we stay up tonight to see what happens."

At sunset, the girls took the mug to the beach. They tried to find the exact spot in the sand where it had been buried. They put it there and hoped children hunting for ghost crabs would leave it alone. After that, they set up the deck for spying. Sydney hung a pair of binoculars around her neck. Bailey had a mini audio recorder in her pocket, a gift Kate had given her for her birthday. The girls had their digital cameras, flashlights, and a notebook and pencils. Now they only had to wait.

Two hours later, Sydney wrote in the notebook:

UFO Log
9 p.m. Kids on beach with flashlights looking for
ghost crabs.

"Can you see if our mug is still there?" Bailey asked.

"I think so," Sydney answered from a folding chair set up near the hammock. "I can only see when one of the kids shines a flashlight in that direction, but so far, it's there."

Bailey settled into a chair next to Sydney's. She opened a bottle of water and sipped. "So did you talk to Beth while I was in the shower?"

"I did," Sydney answered.

"What did Bettyboo say when you told her what was going on?"

"She already knew about it," said Sydney as she took the cap off her water bottle. "McKenzie heard about it from Kate, and she e-mailed Beth. And don't call her Bettyboo. She hates that."

"What did she think about the UFO?" Bailey asked as she put her feet on the deck railing.

"She doesn't believe in UFOs, and she sure doesn't think the Wrights are aliens. She said we should be careful, and she suggested that we look for a logical explanation instead of thinking about UFOs and spirits." Sydney gulped her water.

"What do you think, Syd?" asked Bailey. "Do you think

that God created UFOs?"

Sydney put her feet up on the railing and settled back in her chair. "In my heart of hearts, I don't," she said. "I mean, the Bible says that He created the heavens and the earth and humans and animals, but it doesn't say anything about UFOs."

Bailey looked up at the stars. "I don't want to believe in UFOs and ghosts and stuff, Syd. I don't think that God would create anything bad. But, I know what I saw, and I don't see any other explanation for it." She sighed.

"Tomorrow, Gramps is taking us to the Graveyard of the Atlantic Museum," said Sydney. "Maybe we'll find some answers there. And do you know what, Bailey? We both need to get some sleep. Otherwise we'll be really tired tomorrow. We should watch the beach in shifts. One of us sleeps while the other one watches."

Sydney wrote in the notebook:

> *Sydney—10 p.m. to midnight*
> *Bailey—midnight to 2 a.m.*
> *Sydney—2 a.m. to 4 a.m.*
> *Bailey—4 a.m. to dawn*

At ten o'clock, Bailey stretched out in the hammock and was soon asleep. Sydney had a hard time staying awake. The beach was deserted except for a couple of four-wheelers heading back up north. She watched the moon dodge in and out of clouds. Besides it, the stars, and an occasional airplane flying above the ocean, nothing was in the sky.

When the little travel alarm clock she'd brought on the deck said 12:00, Sydney wrote in the notebook. *Midnight and all is well.* Then she woke Bailey.

"What time is it?" Bailey groaned.

"It's midnight," Sydney said. "I didn't see anything, and it's your turn. Try hard to stay awake. It's easy to get bored." Sydney and Bailey traded places, and Sydney fell asleep.

At first, Bailey scouted every inch of the beach with the binoculars, but she couldn't see anything in the darkness. There was no sound except the waves rolling up on shore. She tried to occupy her mind by singing songs in her head and reciting scripture verses Elizabeth had taught her. Finally, it was 2 a.m. She wrote in the notebook *2 a.m. Nothing to report.*

"Syd?" she said, shaking her friend awake. "It's your turn."

Sydney rolled over in the hammock. "Anything?" she sighed, rubbing the sleep from her eyes.

"Nothing," said Bailey. Then the girls again traded places.

By 3:30 a.m., Sydney was ready to give up. She was bored out of her mind sitting on the deck looking at nothing. She felt her chin hit her chest as she fought off sleep. Then, out of the corner of her eye, she saw something. At least, she thought she did. She thought she saw a flash of bright, white light in the ocean. It flashed briefly and then it disappeared. She waited a few minutes, but there was nothing. Then it flashed again. Five quick bursts of light!

"Bailey! Bailey! Get up. I see something," she urgently whispered.

Bailey rolled so fast in the hammock that she almost sent it flying upside down. "What?" she asked, trying to sit up.

"Sshhh," Sydney whispered. "Look out there." She pointed at the ocean in front of where they sat. After a few seconds, the light flashed again. Sydney noticed that the bursts of light were sometimes long and sometimes short. "It's a code!" she said. "See? Sometimes it flashes longer than others. Write it down, Bailey."

Bailey shone her flashlight onto the notebook paper. "Hide under something," Sydney commanded. "They might see your flashlight."

Bailey dodged under the sleeping bag. As Sydney dictated, Bailey wrote:

> *Short short long*
> *Short short short*
> *SS*
> *LS*
> *LSL. . .*

She wrote for what seemed like forever. Then Sydney stopped dictating. "What's going on?" Bailey asked from under the sleeping bag.

Sydney didn't answer.

"Syd?" Bailey asked. Her muscles tightened and her heart began to race.

"It stopped," Sydney said. "I think you can come out now."

Bailey turned off the flashlight and crawled out from under the sleeping bag. "How weird was that?" she asked.

"Pretty weird," Sydney answered. "Did you get it all written down?"

"Every flash of it," said Bailey proudly. "What do you think it means?"

"I don't know," Sydney answered. "I think we should e-mail it to McKenzie. She's good at analyzing things."

It was just past 4:30 a.m. now, and the beach was pitch-black. It was about the same time that Bailey had seen the UFO the morning before. As the girls looked out at the water, nothing was above it but fading stars. In a little while, the sun would come up over the Atlantic, and another day would begin.

"Hey," Sydney whispered. "Listen."

The girls heard footsteps along the wet sand at the edge of the beach. They came from the south and plodded along rhythmically, passing Sydney's grandparents' beach house, and then stopping just to the north.

"Did you see?" said an older male voice in the darkness.

"It's Captain Swain!" Bailey gasped.

"I saw," a younger male voice answered. "I didn't put the vehicle in the water. Probably best not to until that girl leaves. At least I got my light back." Suddenly, Sydney and Bailey saw their coffee mug flash on and off.

"I think they broke it," said the younger voice.

"That's too bad," said Captain Swain. "We should get out of here before the sun comes up."

Bailey and Sydney sat quietly until they thought the men were gone.

"See?" said Bailey. "The captain is one of them, and they do have a vehicle. I think that they're trying to get back to the Mother Ship, Syd."

"Let's e-mail McKenzie right away," said Sydney. "She won't be up for a few hours, but I know she checks her e-mail first thing in the morning. Maybe she can tell us what the code says before we leave for the museum."

The girls went inside, and Bailey copied the code from her notebook pages to the e-mail document. "There," she said, typing the last *Long short long*. "Let's hope she can figure this out." She hit SEND, and the message flew off through cyberspace.

In less than a minute, they got a reply.

> *I'm up. Our horse, Princess, foaled about*
> *an hour ago. She had a darling colt that we*
> *named Benny. I just came in from the barn.*
> *I'll check out your code and e-mail you back.*

As the sun rose, Bailey and Sydney got dressed and packed their backpacks for the drive to Hatteras. After breakfast, just before Gramps went to get his pickup truck, they checked the e-mail. A message was waiting from McKenzie.

> *It's morse code. It says: I think we're being watched from the Lincoln house. Someone is on the deck with a flashlight.*

Double Trouble

After a long drive down Highway 12 from the top of the Outer Banks to the bottom, the girls and Gramps stopped at the museum, ready to stretch their legs.

"It kind of looks like a shipwreck," said Sydney as she climbed out of her grandfather's truck. She had never been to the Graveyard of the Atlantic Museum, and she had no idea what to expect. The front of the building was outlined in weathered timbers shaped like the hull of a wooden sailing vessel. The building resembled a long, gray ship. Four porthole windows protruded from its roof, reminding Sydney of giant bug eyes.

"I think you'll find some pieces of the ghost ship in here," Gramps said as they walked to the front door.

"Pieces?" said Bailey holding the door for them. "What happened to the rest of it?"

"It stayed aground on the shoals," said Gramps. "After weeks and months of the wind and waves pounding against it, it started to break apart. Then the coast guard dynamited what was left of it."

"Why did they do that?" Bailey asked.

"Because it was a hazard to ships sailing out there. Most of the pieces ended up on the beach. Some of them floated down here to Hatteras Island and got put in the museum. Look over there. There's the capstan. It was used to haul in the ropes on the ship."

The heavy, rusty metal device of the *Carroll A. Deering* rested in front of them. The top was shaped like a lampshade, and a pole came out of the bottom like a rusty old water pipe.

"Was that really a part of the ship?" Sydney asked.

"Yes," said Gramps. "It's the part that raised and lowered the anchors."

Bailey was busy looking at other pieces in the exhibit. She saw timbers from the hull and also pieces of the ship's boom—the long wooden pole that had held up the sails.

"Can you imagine," she said. "This thing was on the ship when all of those sailors disappeared." She felt a shiver run down her spine. "It was there when it happened. The wind probably tore the sails off it when it rocked back and forth on the shoals."

Something ran up the side of her arm and made her jump.

"*Scrape. . .scrape. . .*," Sydney whispered as her fingers tickled Bailey's shoulder.

"That's not funny!" Bailey protested. "If this thing could talk, it would tell us exactly what happened."

"Interested in the *Carroll A. Deering*, are you?" The museum curator walked toward them. He was a short, older man with a bald head and a happy smile.

Gramps shook his hand. "Travis Lincoln," he introduced himself.

"David Jones," said the curator.

"We'd like to know what really happened to the sailors on the ghost ship," said Sydney. "They couldn't have just disappeared. There has to be a logical explanation."

Mr. Jones stood with his elbow resting against a glass cabinet that held more artifacts from the ship. "Well," he said, "that depends on who you talk to. What do you girls think?"

"I'm not sure," said Sydney. "A lot of ships have wrecked off the coast around here. But this one seems so mysterious." She looked inside the glass case at a model of the *Carroll A. Deering*.

"I think they were abducted by aliens!" said Bailey. "I'm almost sure of it."

"Aliens," said Mr. Jones. "Why, that's a theory I haven't heard before. What makes you think it was aliens?"

Bailey waited for a few visitors to pass out of earshot before she answered. "Because we've seen them," she said softly. "With our own eyes."

Sydney frowned at Bailey. "We're not sure what we saw," Sydney said. "We saw some strange lights over the ocean the other night and unusual footprints on the beach."

"Big footprints that looked like waffles!" Bailey added. "And then an alien spacecraft whooshed past us on the beach in the dark. It didn't make a sound, but it hit us with a big puff of air."

Gramps looked confused.

"Young lady, you have quite the imagination," said Mr. Jones. "Let's sit down and talk about this. Maybe I can shed some light on what really happened to the crew of the *Carroll A. Deering*."

He led them to a small, round table and some chairs. The table held a book about the ghost ship and some brochures about the museum. "Now, tell me. What are your names?"

"Sydney Lincoln."

"Bailey Chang."

"Well, Sydney and Bailey, folks have come up with three *logical* explanations. The first one is that the crew abandoned ship. When the coast guard got to the *Carroll A. Deering*, the rope ladder was hanging over the side, and both lifeboats were gone. Someone had run red flares up the rigging to indicate trouble on board."

"Red flares?" said Sydney. "The lights we saw over the ocean the other night were red."

"And sometimes multicolored and flashing," said Bailey. "Maybe it wasn't a spaceship we saw. Maybe it was the ghost ship!"

"I doubt that, Bailey," said Mr. Jones. "Because what's left of the ghost ship is right here."

"You have a point," Bailey said. "But how about a ghost of the ghost ship?"

Mr. Jones smiled and continued. "Now, if the crew did jump ship, they did it in a big hurry, because the galley was set up for a meal, and everything was left behind. However, the theory of abandonment doesn't add up."

"Why?" Sydney asked.

"Because the men were professional sailors who knew what they were doing. In stormy seas, they would be able to steer the ship away from the shoals, but the evidence shows that they sailed right into them!

"Two days before that they'd sailed past the Cape Lookout Lightship, and a crew member reported to the lightkeeper that they had lost both of their anchors, but they'd gotten through the worst of the storm.

"And something was strange about that. Usually a ship's officer makes the report. But on that day the lightkeeper didn't see an officer on deck with the men. Not the captain or a mate or even an engineer. So the officers might have already been missing by then. And the ship ran aground so near the Hatteras Lighthouse that the crew would have been better off to wait for a rescue than to jump ship. The ship didn't seem to be taking on water or anything."

Bailey nervously folded the pages of a brochure. "So maybe the crew member was a ghost?"

"No," said Mr. Jones. "But the crew member might have been up to no good. The officers might have been tied up on board or thrown overboard or even killed."

Gramps had been listening and looking through the book about the *Carroll A. Deering*. "What's your second theory?" he asked.

"Mutiny," said Mr. Jones.

"What does that mean?" Sydney wondered.

"Mutiny means the sailors take over the ship," said Gramps. "If the sailors didn't like the captain, they sometimes found a way to get rid of him."

"That's right," said Mr. Jones. "Captain Willis Wormell was the captain of the *Carroll A. Deering*, and he and his first mate, a man named McLellan, probably didn't get along. Some folks think there was a mutiny at sea. Something strange must have happened because it should have taken the ship about twelve hours to get from Cape Fear to Cape Lookout, but it took six days!"

"Why so long?" Bailey asked.

"No one knows," Mr. Jones answered. "It's part of the mystery. But some of the ship's charts were found in the wreck. After the ship got past Cape Fear, none of the entries in the charts were in Captain Wormell's handwriting. Three sets of boots were found in the captain's cabin, but none of them were the captain's. Some folks think he was killed and thrown overboard."

"Was he?" Sydney asked.

"No one knows," said Mr. Jones.

"Boy," Bailey said. "There sure is a lot of stuff that no

one knows. So it still could be aliens, right?"

"I doubt it," said the curator. "Plenty of things point to a mutiny, but there's no evidence, and if you know anything about solving a mystery, you know you need evidence."

"Oh, we know that!" said Sydney. "Our group of friends, the Camp Club Girls, have solved several mysteries now."

Gramps smiled. "The girls and their friends from summer camp have quite the reputation for solving mysteries. You wouldn't believe some of the adventures they've had."

"I can only imagine," said Mr. Jones.

"I suppose it could have been mutiny," said Sydney. "But without evidence, we can't make that conclusion. If McLellan killed the officers and the crew, he had to do something with the bodies, and they were never found. Were there any signs of a fight on board?"

"No," said Mr. Jones. "Wormell was a big man and could have put up quite a fight. And *both* lifeboats were missing, and that doesn't make sense if McLellan was the only one left on board."

"That is weird," said Bailey. "But there's not enough evidence in either of those theories to convince me the crew members weren't abducted by aliens."

"Is there evidence to convince you that they *were*?" Sydney asked.

Bailey bit her lower lip. "No," she confessed. "What's the third theory?"

"Pirates," said Mr. Jones.

"Like Blackbeard?" Sydney asked.

"No," Mr. Jones replied. "He died long before then. But pirates still sailed in the sea. One theory is that pirates took over another ship named the *Hewitt*, killed everyone, and then threw a tarp over the ship's nameplate. So, if anyone saw the ship, they wouldn't know which one it was.

"And shortly after the *Carroll A. Deering* passed the Cape Lookout Lightship, another ship sailed by—"

"What's a lightship, anyhow?" Bailey interrupted.

"A lightship is a special ship equipped with a really bright light," said Mr. Jones. "Lightships are used in places where a lighthouse can't be built. They're moored off the coast in places that are dangerous for ships to navigate." He found a picture of a lightship in the book on the table and showed it to the girls.

"Maybe the signals we saw were from a lightship?" Bailey said.

"Signals?" said Gramps.

"We think we saw someone flashing a white light in Morse code early this morning," said Sydney. "It was in the ocean straight out from our house at around four o'clock."

"What were you girls doing up at four o'clock?" asked Gramps.

"Watching for UFOs," said Bailey.

"Oh, girls," said Gramps, shaking his head. "There are no such things as UFOs. . . Mr. Jones, please tell us more about the *Hewitt*."

"Well, that second ship, the one that was following the *Deering*, was hailed by the lightship at Cape Lookout. Usually, someone on board would shout a report, like the crew member from the *Deering* did. Only, this time, the ship sailed right on by without reporting. The lightship keeper said he couldn't find a nameplate on the ship, so no one knows, but it could have been the *Hewitt*."

"Another unknown," said Bailey.

"The theory is that pirates killed everyone on the *Hewitt* and then stole the vessel. After that, they attacked the *Deering*, killed its crew, and stole anything valuable. Then they transferred their treasure to the *Hewitt*, steered the *Carroll A. Deering* in the direction of the shoals, and jumped ship."

Sydney was fidgeting with her cornrows again, like she often did when she was thinking. "But what about the bodies of all those sailors? They were never found."

"They never were," Mr. Jones agreed. "And some of their remains would have probably appeared sooner or later."

"Except that we found one of their bones on the beach," said Bailey.

"What?" Gramps exclaimed.

"I stepped on a bone in the sand, and Sydney said it was part of a dead sailor."

"I did not!" said Sydney. "I was telling you a ghost story. The bone was probably left from someone's barbeque lunch."

Mr. Jones chuckled. "It sounds like you girls are having quite the time up there in Corolla."

Sydney remembered what she had been thinking about before Bailey had mentioned the bone. "What happened to the *Hewitt*?" she asked.

"Well," said Mr. Jones. "That's another great mystery. It disappeared around the same time the *Carroll A. Deering* was found stuck in the shoals. It was never heard from again."

"Another ghost ship!" said Bailey. "It sounds like there's no more evidence to support those theories than mine: I still think they were abducted by aliens."

Mr. Jones sighed. "I guess I can't argue with you, Bailey. But I don't believe in UFOs."

"Me neither," said Gramps.

Bailey looked to Sydney for support.

"I don't know," Sydney said. "We've seen and heard some strange things lately and haven't found any logical explanations."

"You're the Camp Club Girls!" Mr. Jones said. "Be good detectives, and see if you can find an explanation for your UFOs. If nothing else, you'll come up with some good theories. Who knows, maybe fifty years from now, people will discuss your UFO theories the way we just discussed the theories about the *Deering*."

The girls thanked Mr. Jones for his time. Then they went to explore the rest of the museum.

Bailey was excited to see a lighthouse exhibit, including

a model of the Cape Hatteras black-and-white striped lighthouse. She enjoyed looking at the exhibits for each of the lighthouses on the Outer Banks, including the Currituck Beach Lighthouse, in Corolla.

"Hey, Kate would be interested in this," said Sydney. "When the lighthouse we climbed was first built, it didn't have electricity. The lighthouse keeper had to rotate the lens at the top of the tower by hand so the light appeared to flash."

Bailey looked at a diagram of the lighthouse showing all of its parts. "If Kate had lived back then, she'd have found some sort of high-tech gadget to make it easier. Hey, if there was no electricity, where did the light come from?"

Sydney read the caption under a picture. "It came from a giant oil lamp," she said. "The lens was rotated with a system of weights, sort of the way a grandfather clock works. The lighthouse keeper or his assistant had to crank the weights by hand every two and a half hours. Look, here's a picture."

Bailey studied the old, yellowed photo of the lighthouse keeper cranking the weights. "Captain Swain!"

"What?" said Sydney.

"It says here, CAPTAIN NATHAN SWAIN ROTATES THE LENS ON THE CURRITUCK BEACH LIGHTHOUSE, 1910. Sydney, that's a picture of him. It's Captain Swain!"

Sydney looked carefully at the photo. "It does sort of look like him," she said, "but it can't be, because this picture was taken one hundred years ago."

"It's him," Bailey insisted. "He's a ghost."

"What are you girls so interested in?" asked Gramps. He had been looking at another exhibit across the room.

"Just this picture of the Currituck Beach lighthouse keeper," said Sydney. "He looks like someone we saw there the other day."

"There's a whole book about the lighthouse keepers over there," said Gramps, pointing across the room. "Maybe you can find him in there."

Bailey and Sydney found the book *Lightkeepers of the Outer Banks* on a table near the exhibits. Sydney looked in the table of contents and found "Currituck Beach Lighthouse." She turned to page 87 and found a list of lightkeepers beginning in 1875. Sydney read them aloud, "Burris, Simmons, Shinnault, Scott, Simpson, Hinnant, another Simmons. . . Here he is—Nathan H. Swain! He was the lighthouse keeper from 1905 until 1920."

"Is there a picture of him?" Bailey asked, looking over Sydney's shoulder.

"No," she answered. "But there's a footnote." She turned to the back of the book, and there she found a photograph of an old newspaper article, "CAPTAIN NATHAN H. SWAIN RETIRES AS KEEPER OF THE CURRITUCK BEACH LIGHTHOUSE."

There was a picture, a close-up of the captain wearing his uniform. Sydney caught her breath. "It's him!"

"Oh my," Bailey said. "He really is a ghost!"

Theories

After their day in Hatteras, the girls were relaxing in their room. Sydney was on the bed studying a photocopy of the Captain Swain article. She even used a magnifying glass to look at his picture better.

"This photo is a little blurry. It sure does look like our captain," she said. "But it can't be the same man."

Bailey sat at the desk painting her fingernails with a light blue nail polish called Gonna' Getchu Blue.

"He's a ghost!" she insisted. "That explains why he disappeared at the lighthouse and on the beach the other morning."

"Yeah, but what about *this* morning?" said Sydney. "We heard him talking with that other guy on the beach—"

"The alien," Bailey added, blowing on her nails.

Sydney got up and slid open the glass doors letting the warm ocean breeze rush into the room. "Think about this, Bailey. You're telling me that a ghost was on the beach this morning, and he was talking to a space alien. Do you know how crazy that sounds?"

Bailey tightened the cap on the nail polish bottle. "Okay, so do you have another explanation? If he's not a ghost, how do you explain that the Captain Swain in the newspaper article isn't the same guy?"

"I don't know yet," said Sydney. "But I'm going to find out." She sat down on the bed and opened her laptop. "I'm going to e-mail the girls everything we know so far, and if we work together we'll get to the bottom of this."

Sydney wrote an e-mail to the Camp Club Girls. She included her list of facts:

1. *Before Bailey arrived, there were reports of strange lights over the Atlantic Ocean near the Outer Banks.*
2. *On Bailey's first night, she saw flashing red lights over the water.*
3. *The next day, after we climbed the lighthouse, Captain Swain seemed to disappear.*
4. *That afternoon, we found the mysterious mug on the beach.*
5. *Early yesterday morning, we saw a UFO. We heard a whirring noise, but then the sound quit. Something rushed past us on the beach with a puff of air. It left waffle-like footprints. Then we ran into Captain Swain on the beach. He seemed to disappear in a hurry again.*

6. *Later, we went to watch Nate Wright cluster balloon. The words on the Wrights' bus spelled "Roswell" backward.*

7. *In the afternoon, the mug started flashing, so we put it back on the beach where we found it.*

8. *Early this morning, someone out in the ocean was using a flashing light to send morse code. The message said:* I think we're being watched from the Lincoln house. Someone is on the deck with a flashlight.

9. *We heard Captain Swain on the beach talking to another guy. The guy said he wasn't going to put the "vehicle" in the water until Bailey left. He also said the mug was his and that we broke it. He took it with him.*

10. *Today, we went to the graveyard of the Atlantic Museum. We found an old newspaper article with a picture of a guy named Captain Nathan Swain. He looks just like our Captain Swain. But the picture was taken 100 years ago!*

So, Camp Club Girls, who is this man, and what are the mysterious lights over the ocean?

Sydney and Bailey

Sydney attached a copy of the article with the picture of Captain Swain. "There," she said. "Now we'll see what the girls come up with."

Bailey was looking at her nails, "Do you like this color," she asked, "or should I try Sparkle Me Purple?"

"I like the blue," said Sydney. "You know, I just remembered something. Didn't the captain say he'd climbed the lighthouse before?"

"Yeah," Bailey answered. "He said, 'I climbed these stairs a lot back in the day,' or something like that—which would make sense if he was the lighthouse keeper. I mean, they had to rotate that thingy by hand to make the light work, right? Didn't they have to do that every couple of hours? So he would've climbed those stairs lots of times. He's a ghost, Syd. Admit it."

Sydney sat fidgeting with her cornrows. "Remember what Mr. Jones said? We should rule out all the other theories before we decide that he's a ghost or an alien or a mystery that we can't explain." She picked up Bailey's bottle of blue nail polish and shook it.

"So what's your theory?" asked Bailey.

"Well, I thought that maybe our captain was the son of the man in the article." Sydney opened the bottle and brushed some Gonna' Getchu Blue onto her thumbnail. "But then I read the article again, and Captain Nathan Swain only had one child, a daughter named Nellie." She held her right hand out to look at the color.

"Any other theories?" Bailey asked.

"Not yet," said Sydney. "How about you?"

"Maybe he just happens to look exactly like the guy in the photograph and just *happens* to be a captain, too, and just *happens* to have the same last name."

"Are you being sarcastic?" Sydney asked, wiping the polish.

"Of course I am," said Bailey. "There's maybe room for one coincidence, but not three."

Sydney chose a bottle of pale Tickle Me Pink nail polish and began brushing it onto her nails. She was almost done when her cell phone rang. "Bailey, will you get that, please?" she asked. "My nails are wet."

Bailey got Sydney's phone out of her backpack. "It's a text message from Mac. It says: I'm setting up a group chat for tonight. We need to discuss this!"

"Great," Sydney said. "We need all the help we can get."

●—●—●

When Bailey and Sydney logged into the chatroom after supper, the other Camp Club Girls were waiting.

> McKenzie: *We were talking before you got here. Do you know much about your Captain Swain, the one from the lighthouse?*

Sydney and Bailey sat next to each other on Syd's bed.

Sydney: *No, we didn't really get to know him at all. He walked up the stairs with us and helped Bailey get over her fear of heights. Then, once we were up there, he left, or something, and we didn't see him go.*

McKenzie: *What does he look like?*

Sydney: *He's about as tall as I am and sort of round. he had a gray beard and was dressed like a sea captain. He had on a blue captain's cap and a blue, heavy jacket with shiny buttons.*

"Don't forget about the dog," said Bailey.

Sydney: *And he has a shaggy black dog about the size of biscuit. Named McTavish. When we saw the captain on the beach, he wore a dark blue jogging suit with a coast guard emblem on the sleeve.*

"And he talks about God," Bailey reminded her.

Sydney: *And he talks about God.*

Elizabeth: *What does he say about God?*

Sydney: *He quotes the Bible and says that he and God are talking out loud.*

Elizabeth: *Then he must be a Christian. And
I think that's your best reason to believe
that he's not a ghost.*

Bailey borrowed the laptop from Sydney.

Bailey: *Why?*
Elizabeth: *Because when Christians die,
their souls go to heaven. The Bible says
in 2 Corinthians 5:8 that when we're
absent from our bodies, we're present with
the Lord.*
McKenzie: *So we know your captain is
somehow involved with the lights, right?*
Bailey: *He had something to do with whoever
was flashing the morse code this morning.
But we don't know for sure that he had
anything to do with the strange lights
flashing over the water.*
Alexis: *What do you know about the cluster
ballooning guys, the ones with the Roswell
bus?*

Bailey looked at Sydney and shrugged her shoulders.
She didn't really know much about the Wrights except
what she'd heard from Sydney, her grandparents, and the
Kessler twins. She gave the laptop back to Sydney.

Sydney carried it over to the desk and turned on a lamp in the room. It was nearly dark outside, and it had begun to rain. Bailey pulled up a chair and joined her.

> Sydney: *They're related to the Wright Brothers. You remember them, don't you? They invented the airplane, and they made their first flight down the coast from here near Kitty Hawk. Nate is a distant cousin or something. He has a son named Drake, but everyone around here calls him Digger. I think he's around fifteen.*
>
> Kate: *How cool is that? You actually* know *relatives of the Wright Brothers!*
>
> Sydney: *I don't know them. They keep to themselves. The only time anyone sees Mr. Wright is when he's testing an invention, and Digger only comes out when no one else is around or when he's helping his dad.*
>
> Elizabeth: *Why do they call him Digger?*

Sydney got up and slid the glass doors closed. It was raining hard now, and the beach was empty. It was too rainy for ghost crab hunting, or anything else for that matter. She sat back at the desk.

> Sydney: *Because he picks up junk on the*

beach. I'm not sure what exactly, but it's usually stuff that washes up on the shore. The other morning, Bailey and I saw him stuffing things into his backpack. Sometimes he walks along the water with a strange cart. He fills it with driftwood and stuff, but if he sees anyone coming, he leaves.

Bailey took the computer from Sydney.

Bailey: *I've seen him a couple of times. He's kind of cute. He's tall, thin, and tan, and he has shaggy blond hair. He looks like a surfer.*

McKenzie: *Mmm. What's Mr. Wright like?*

Sydney: *Imagine Santa Claus on a bad day. He's older with a sunburned face, a scruffy white beard, and white hair that hangs over his collar. He always wears a red baseball cap and bib overalls.*

"And cowboy boots," Bailey added.

Sydney: *And cowboy boots. Mr. Wright is an inventor. At least that's what people say. He doesn't talk much. This summer,*

> he's experimenting with cluster ballooning
> as a green way of transportation.
> Elizabeth: *So in the future, we'll all travel in
> chairs powered by balloons?*
> Sydney: *If Mr. Wright has his way.*
> Alexis: *I think your captain fits in with the
> Wrights, but I can't figure out the missing
> piece. So far, we have a 100-year-old
> Captain Swain, a younger Captain Swain
> who looks like him, a kid who picks up
> junk on the beach, and an inventor who
> flies in a chair powered by balloons.*

Bailey was busy thinking. She licked her lips and borrowed the laptop from Sydney.

> Bailey: *Maybe they're all modern pirates. Mr.
> Jones, at the museum, said pirates were
> still around when the ghost ship
> disappeared. Maybe Nate Wright has
> invented a flying machine that scopes out
> ships at sea. Maybe it has a big hook that
> snatches the cargo. Then, he drops it on
> the beach, and Digger picks it up. I'm still
> not sure what the ghost captain does, though.*
> McKenzie: *Maybe they're divers and
> scavengers. Divers find old shipwrecks*

and rummage through them looking for
stuff to sell. Aren't there tons of old wrecks
off the shores of the Outer Banks?

The rain was falling harder now. It drummed on the roof over Sydney and Bailey's room.

"That's the best theory yet," Sydney said to Bailey. "Don't you think so?"

Bailey was chewing her lower lip. "It makes sense," she answered. "But what about the captain? We still don't know who he is, or how he's involved."

Sydney: *We like your theory, Mac, but how*
  does Captain Swain fit in?
Kate: *And what about that other guy on the*
  beach, the one the captain was talking to
  this morning. Do you have any theories
  about him?
Elizabeth: *A kid's young voice, or a man's*
  young voice?
Sydney: *A young man's voice. Lots of boys are*
  around here. It could have been anyone.
Kate: *Could it have been Digger?*
McKenzie: *I was just going to suggest that.*
Alexis: *I was thinking it, too.*

The rain was pelting the windows in the guest room,

and Bailey sat watching the water stream down the panes. "What do you think?" Sydney asked her. "Could the voice we heard on the beach this morning have been Drake Wright?"

"I suppose it could," said Bailey. "The only time I've heard him is when he yelled 'Get back' yesterday morning, and I don't really remember what he sounded like."

Sydney sighed. "Well, that would connect the Wrights with the captain. It's an idea worth exploring."

> Sydney: *We're not sure, but it might have been. We need to investigate.*
> Alexis: *The scavenger theory is beginning to make sense. But we still need to figure out Captain Swain. Do you know anyone else who knows him?*

Sydney leaned back in her chair and thought.

> Sydney: *I don't know* many people *in the village. I only go there when I ride my bike. I like to get ice cream at a little restaurant there and hang out by the lighthouse sometimes. I've never seen the captain before, but I could ask around and see if anyone knows him.*

Bailey's face lit up. "Hey," she said. "What about the lighthouse lady?"

"Huh?" Sydney asked.

"You know. The lady who gave us the sticker books. You asked her if she'd seen the captain coming down the stairs, and she said, 'Captain Swain.' I remember. She used his name."

Sydney remembered, too. "You're right! She did use his name, didn't she? Then she definitely knows who he is. She's new at the lighthouse this summer, so I didn't even think about her. Good work, Bailey."

> Sydney: *Bailey just remembered the lady who takes care of the lighthouse talked about the captain, so we'll go there tomorrow and ask her.*
>
> McKenzie: *That's great! If you can find out about him, you'll be closer to solving the mystery of the lights over the ocean.*
>
> Elizabeth: *I know he's definitely not the ghost of Captain Swain. I'll pray tonight that you find out your beach isn't haunted by ghosts or being invaded by aliens.*
>
> Alexis: *Keep us posted. Good-bye for now from Sacramento.*
>
> McKenzie: *And from big sky country.*
>
> Kate: *And from Philly.*

"Well," said Sydney, shutting down her laptop. "It's a good theory that they might be scavenging old shipwrecks." She turned off the desk lamp.

"I guess so," said Bailey. "Maybe the lighthouse lady will have some answers about Captain Swain when we go there tomorrow."

Camp Club Spies

"It's locked," Sydney said. She stood on the lighthouse porch and pulled the door handle. "Maybe storms are coming."

Bailey laid her bike in the grass next to Sydney's and took off her backpack. "I don't think so. I watched the weather this morning. We're in for a bright, sunny day." She threw her backpack on the ground next to Sydney's.

"Everything's still wet from the rain last night," Sydney observed. "There are puddles all over the place."

"And mud," Bailey added. "Look at the mess you're leaving." She pointed to the footprints going up the front steps to the door.

Sydney lifted each foot and checked the bottoms of her tennis shoes. They were wet, but clean. "It's not my mess," she said. "Someone else has been here." She knocked on the lighthouse door, but no one answered.

"The footprints are too big to be the lighthouse lady's," Bailey said. "They're more like boot prints."

Sydney knocked again.

"So now what?" Bailey asked.

"Maybe there's a back door," Sydney replied. She walked down the steps and disappeared around the side of the lighthouse with Bailey close behind.

The lighthouse was attached to a small, brick house. The girls discovered that it had no back door. Instead, where a back door would be, the house was connected to the tower. The sides of the house had several tall windows flanked by green shutters. Each narrow window was made up of ten little panes of glass.

"I wish I could look inside," said Sydney. "But the windows are too high." She jumped up trying to peek in, but still wasn't tall enough.

"Boost me up," said Bailey.

"Huh?"

"Boost me up." Bailey stepped behind Sydney. She grabbed her shoulders and swung her legs around Sydney's hips. Then she stretched her neck to see through the window. "I'm not high enough," she said. Bailey put her feet back on the ground. "Can you boost me up on your shoulders?"

"I can try," said Sydney. She bent over. Bailey climbed onto her shoulders and wrapped her arms around Sydney's neck. Then Sydney stood up and teetered against Bailey's weight. "Can you see anything?" she asked.

"The sun's reflecting off the glass," Bailey answered. "Move me closer."

Sydney took a giant step forward while trying to balance Bailey and keep herself from falling.

Bailey let go of Sydney's neck and rested her hands on each side of the window. She pressed her nose against the glass. The room she was looking at was the office.

"Nobody's in there," she said. "The blue WAIT HERE TO CLIMB sign is in the middle of the room, so the lighthouse must be closed. Hey wait. Someone is moving in there. I see a shadow." For a few seconds, Bailey said nothing. Then she pushed herself off Sydney's shoulders and fell to the ground. "Run!" she said. She got up from the ground and scrambled with Sydney toward a grove of trees.

"What did you see?" Sydney asked as they slipped behind a big evergreen tree.

"It was Nate Wright," Bailey answered. "He had a really long chain and was heading for the curvy staircase. I think he might have seen me."

"Shhhh," said Sydney. "Look."

Nate Wright came around the side of the lighthouse. He was dressed in his bib overalls and red cap, and he looked as scruffy as ever. He stopped and looked left and right. Then as the girls watched through the thick, needled branches, he took off his cap, scratched his head, and walked back toward the front of the lighthouse.

"I think he saw you," Sydney whispered. "I think he was looking around for you."

"Yeah, but he has no idea who I am," said Bailey. "Unless

he recognized me from when we watched him cluster ballooning on the beach."

"I doubt it. He was too busy to pay any attention to the crowd."

"So now what?" Bailey asked.

"We find a safe place to watch, far enough away, where we can keep our eyes on the front door. There's no other exit from the building."

Bailey stepped out of the grove of trees and began walking toward the lighthouse. Sydney grabbed her arm and pulled her back. "Where are you going?"

"We have to get our bikes and backpacks," said Bailey.

"Not now," Sydney told her. "We should leave them there. Otherwise, he might see us."

Bailey sighed. "But if we leave them, it's a dead giveaway that we're here."

"We have to take that chance," Sydney answered. "Let's double back through these trees. We'll end up on Schoolhouse Road by the Village Bar-B-Q. Then we can cross the street and watch the lighthouse from there."

Bailey followed Sydney through the trees, along a winding footpath, and over to Schoolhouse Road. They made a wide circle to avoid walking close to the lighthouse. Then they found a park bench not far from the lighthouse museum shop. From there, they could see the lighthouse and its front door.

"Look," said Bailey, pointing upward. "He's up on the lookout."

From where the girls sat, Mr. Wright appeared to be a tiny figure. His red baseball cap made him easy to see. His back was to the heavy, iron railing, and he seemed to be busy doing something, but they couldn't tell what.

"I wish I had my binoculars," Sydney said. "They're in my backpack."

"No problem," said Bailey. "I'll get them."

Before Sydney could stop her, Bailey was running up the brick path toward the lighthouse door. With lightning speed, she snatched Sydney's bike and backpack. Then she hurried back to Sydney.

"There," she said, handing her the backpack. "Mission accomplished." She laid Sydney's bike on the ground.

Sydney unzipped a deep pocket on the outside of the backpack and pulled out her binoculars. Then she put the eyepiece to her eyes, pointed the lens at the lookout, and focused.

"He's pulling on something," she said. "Wait. It's that chain you saw. He's pulling it through the little doorway that leads out to the lookout. Boy, is it ever long! He's already got a bunch of it lying on the floor up there."

"Why do you think he's doing that?" Bailey asked. She squinted, trying to see.

"Beats me," said Sydney. She handed the binoculars to Bailey.

Just then, a rumble came from Schoolhouse Road. Sydney looked in that direction and saw a man driving a small, green tractor. The tractor pulled an open trailer that held a tall wooden crate. The tractor left the road and turned onto the lighthouse grounds. Sydney watched it weave around the trees and onto the path near where they sat. Then she recognized the driver.

"Bailey, turn away!" she hissed.

"What?" asked Bailey.

"Turn and face me, right now!"

The urgency in Sydney's voice made Bailey do as she was told. She put the binoculars on her lap, turned her body sideways on the bench, and looked at Sydney's back.

"Syd, why are we sitting like this?" she asked.

By now the tractor had passed them and was moving toward the front of the lighthouse. Sydney turned and looked at Bailey. "I didn't want him to recognize us," she said.

"Who to recognize us?" Bailey wondered.

"The man driving the tractor was Captain Swain!" said Sydney.

The captain was barely recognizable without his navy blue clothing. He was dressed in a pair of jeans and a black tee shirt. The only thing that made Sydney sure that it was him was his neat, gray beard and the captain's cap on his head. He drove the tractor to the lighthouse steps and stopped. As the girls watched, Captain Swain walked to the front door, took out a key, and entered.

"Look, he has a key to the lighthouse," said Sydney.

"That's strange," Bailey replied. She handed the

binoculars to Sydney. "Why would he have a key? Maybe it's a skeleton key, the kind that opens any old door."

"Hi, Sydney!"

"Hi, Bailey!"

The Kessler twins came from behind them. Each was walking with a tandem bike.

"I didn't know you guys were going to the Village this morning," said Carolyn.

"Me neither," said Marilyn. "What are you doing with those binoculars?"

Sydney wasn't about to tell the Kesslers what was going on. They had a reputation for not being able to keep a secret.

"Sometimes I like bird watching," she said, which was totally true.

"Bird watching!" Marilyn exclaimed.

"Sydney's a nature nut," said Bailey. "At Discovery Lake Camp she was the only camper who knew about every animal in the woods and every bird in the sky. What are you guys doing here?"

"We're going to pick up our brothers," said Carolyn.

"We stopped at the Bar-B-Q first to get root beer," said Marilyn. "Are you guys going to the crab fest tonight?" She rested her bike against the bench where Sydney and Bailey sat.

"What's a crab fest?" Sydney asked. Captain Swain came out of the lighthouse now, and Sydney nudged Bailey with her elbow.

Sydney watched the captain as he unhitched the gate on

the trailer. Mr. Wright was still on the lookout, but without using her binoculars Sydney couldn't tell what he was up to.

"So are you going?" said Marilyn.

"Where?" Sydney asked. She was busy watching the captain as he climbed into the trailer and took the straps off the crate.

"To the crab fest!" Marilyn replied.

"Sydney asked you what it is," Carolyn reminded her.

"Oh, yeah," Marilyn said. "The Village is having a crab boil tonight."

"The restaurant is sponsoring it," Carolyn added. "They'll have a big crab dinner—"

"With corn, potatoes, deep-fried onion petals, and homemade cherry pie," said Marilyn.

"And ice cream!" Carolyn said. "And they're having bands and some carnival games. It's to raise money for the lighthouse renovation. That's a good cause, don't you think?" She picked up her tandem and held onto the front handlebars.

"Uh-huh," said Sydney. She noticed that Mr. Wright looked even busier up on the lookout. She nudged Bailey again, and Bailey nudged her back.

"So are you going?" asked Marilyn picking up her bike.

"I'm not sure yet," said Sydney. "We'll let you know." Her fingers were wrapped around the binoculars in her lap. She couldn't wait to look through them to see what Nate Wright was up to.

"It sounds like fun," Bailey said halfheartedly. "So maybe we'll see you later then."

"Okay," said Marilyn, hopping onto her bike and shoving off. "See you later!"

Carolyn got onto her bike and followed, "See you later," she echoed.

Sydney sighed with relief. "I'm glad they're gone."

She already had the binoculars to her eyes. "He's lowering the chain down to the captain." Mr. Wright had the big chain wrapped around a heavy wheel-like machine up on the lookout. He was lowering one end of it to Captain Swain who was standing inside the trailer. Sydney noticed a big hook on the end of the chain.

"What do you think's in the box?" she asked.

"I don't know," Bailey replied. "It's about as tall as I am, so it must be big."

"Too big to carry up that spiral staircase," said Sydney.

Bailey watched. "You know, Syd, I'm wondering where the lighthouse lady is. Do you think she knows what's going on in there?"

"I don't know," Sydney answered. "Captain Swain just hooked the chain onto the crate."

From somewhere above them came the whirring of an engine. Bailey looked up expecting to see a small plane flying overhead, but nothing was in the sky.

"What's that noise?" she asked.

"It's coming from the lookout," said Sydney as the crate

113

lifted off the trailer and up into the air. "Mr. Wright has a gasoline-powered pulley up there. That's what's making the noise. It's lifting the crate to the top of the lighthouse."

Sydney and Bailey took turns with the binoculars watching the crate rise. Mr. Wright guided it over the top of the railing and set it on the narrow floor. Once it was safely secured, Captain Swain went inside.

"He's going up by Mr. Wright," said Sydney. "Now's a good time to get your bike. You watch, and I'll go this time." She handed the binoculars to Bailey before heading up the narrow brick path. When Sydney got near the door, she heard two men talking inside. She hid next to the porch and listened. One of the voices she recognized as the captain's. The other was the younger voice they'd heard on the beach.

"She's locked up in our equipment shed," said the young man.

"Good," said Captain Swain. "A job well-done, Drake, a job well-done."

Digger! Sydney thought. *He was on the beach with the captain.*

"I've taken care of all the paperwork," Captain Swain continued. "You won't have to keep it a secret anymore. Tonight, I'll help you fix the problem with the rudder. Then you're on your way."

"I'm nervous about people seeing it," Drake answered.

"My boy, an anxious heart weighs a man down," said the

captain. "Just me and God talking to you."

Sydney grabbed Bailey's bike and rushed back to the bench. "Drake's in there, too!" she told Bailey. "They have someone locked in their equipment shed!"

"Who?" Bailey asked.

"I don't know," Sydney answered. "Drake said, 'She's locked up safe in our equipment shed.' "

"The lighthouse lady!" Bailey gasped. "They've kidnapped her."

"I didn't think of that," Sydney answered as she laid Bailey's bike on the grass. "Do you really think they've kidnapped her? And why would they do that?"

"What else did they say?" Bailey asked as she handed the binoculars to Sydney.

"Tonight, the captain is helping them fix some sort of problem, and then they're leaving. The captain said that after that they'll be on their way." Sydney sat down next to Bailey.

"See," said Bailey. "I *am* right. They're aliens, and Captain Swain is helping them. They're taking the lighthouse lady with them. She's being abducted by aliens!"

Sydney watched while the Wrights and Captain Swain pried open the wooden crate. "Bailey, I still believe that there's a logical explanation for all this. I just don't know what it is yet."

Bailey sighed. "So now what?"

"I think we need to go to the crab fest tonight. We can

go to the Wright's place when it's dark out, and then we can see what's going on."

Up on the lookout, the men were lifting something out of the crate.

"It's a big telescope!" Sydney said as she handed the binoculars to Bailey.

"They're setting it up," Bailey observed. "They're attaching it to the railing up there. Now the captain is looking through it. He's looking out at the ocean." Bailey handed the binoculars back to Sydney. "I think they put it there so they can watch for the Mother Ship tonight."

Sydney didn't even bother to argue with Bailey about the alien idea. Mr. Wright was lowering the chain, and the empty crate dropped to the ground.

"I think they're leaving," said Sydney.

The girls waited to see what would happen next. Mr. Wright and Digger were the first to come out the front door. They walked across the grass to Schoolhouse Road. Then they turned west toward home. The captain came out next. He locked the door behind him and started down the front porch stairs. When he got to the bottom, he stopped.

"Oh no, my backpack!" said Bailey.

Captain Swain picked up the backpack and read the name on its ID tag: BAILEY CHANG. He looked around. Then he set the backpack on the lighthouse steps and drove away on his tractor.

Questions

Sydney's grandparents agreed that the crab fest would be a fun activity for the girls. As they got ready to leave, Bailey flung her backpack over her shoulders.

"At least he didn't take it with him," she said. She was talking about what had happened that morning when Captain Swain saw her backpack by the lighthouse porch.

"I'd feel better if your name wasn't on it," said Sydney. "If Mr. Wright saw you looking through the window and described you to the captain, he might have put two and two together."

"I didn't think of that," Bailey answered.

"Let me check in and see if any of the girls have sent anything," Sydney said.

Sure enough, when she logged on the computer, she found a couple of notes on the private wall of the Camp Club Girls Web site.

Alexis: *I watched an old TV show today and it made me think about your problem with the identity of Captain Swain. On the show, two grown-up cousins looked so much alike that they were mistaken for twins. Sometimes that happens—a family resemblance may be strong in several people, even if they're not brothers and sisters, or children of the person they look like. We know the original Captain Swain didn't have any sons, so your Captain Swain couldn't be his son. But maybe he's a cousin of the original Captain Swain or something.*

Kate: *I've been thinking about Captain Swain, too. Bailey, I'm like Beth—I don't believe in ghosts. And ghosts don't own property—according to the law, no dead people can own property. But I looked on the Internet and found that there's a Captain Swain with the address of Duck, North Carolina. When I Googled Duck, I found out it's just south of Corolla. So it sounds like your Captain Swain is a legitimate resident of the area!*

"Sounds like one mystery is solved, anyway," Sydney said.

"I don't know," Bailey said. "It sounds convincing, but I think I'm going to confront Captain Swain and ask him for myself."

Sydney grinned. Sometimes Bailey was so dramatic!

"Well, come on," Sydney said. "Maybe you'll see him at the crab fest and you can ask him there!"

By the time the girls arrived in Corolla Village, the sun had just set. A crowd had gathered at the Corolla Village Bar-B-Q where glowing paper lanterns were strung from tree to tree. On the front lawn, steam rose from a huge, black pot over a fire. Two cooks from the restaurant dumped buckets full of crabs into the boiling water. Then they added Old Bay seasoning, ears of corn, onions, and small new potatoes.

"Yum, that smells good," said Bailey. On a small stage, at the edge of the parking lot, the Wild Horse Band was playing a tune. Bailey grabbed Sydney's hands and swung her around in time with the music.

"Woo-hoo! Let's hear it for the crab fest!" Bailey squealed.

As the girls spun, Sydney glimpsed the Kessler twins arriving with their brothers and mom and dad.

"The twins are here," she told Bailey when the music stopped. "We probably have to hang out with them, but we need to get away to investigate the Wrights' place. Listen, don't say anything about what we're up to, okay? They can't keep a secret."

"Have they seen us?" Bailey asked.

"I don't think so," said Sydney.

"Then why don't we go over to the Wrights' now? We can see what's going on and then come back here and hang out with the twins."

Sydney agreed, and soon she and Bailey were walking up Schoolhouse Road in the direction of the sound. When they got to Persimmon Street, they saw a narrow, sandy road marked PRIVATE DRIVE.

"This must be it," said Sydney. She remembered her grandmother saying the Wrights' lived on a wooded private road off Persimmon. "Gram knows a potter who lives on this road, and the Wright's place is just beyond hers. It's at the end of the drive, I think."

The girls turned onto the sandy lane and walked along the edge of the woods.

"I wish we had a flashlight," said Bailey. The only light came from porch lights along the way. The road was barely wide enough for two cars to pass, and it was deserted. Either all the residents were at the crab fest or they were inside their houses.

Bailey noticed that these houses weren't like most others on the Outer Banks. These were old-fashioned, two-story cottages with narrow front porches and gabled roofs. They looked like they had been there forever.

Who-who-whooooo-who-who. A great-horned owl called from a distant tree.

"I feel like I'm back at Discovery Lake Camp," said Bailey. "This place is spooky. It's so dark and deserted. Syd, are you sure you want to do this?"

"Look. Here's the potter's house," said Sydney. At the

edge of the road, an old, tin mailbox sat atop a lovely statue of a mermaid. The name on the box said WILMA HEISER, POTTERY PLUS.

"The Wrights' place has to be over there." She pointed ahead to a sharp bend in the road.

"Listen!"

A loud rumble came from behind them. Some sort of vehicle had just turned off Persimmon Street and onto the private drive.

"Someone's coming. We have to hide!"

Sydney grabbed Bailey and pulled her behind some tall bushes in the potter's front yard. They could see the road.

Thud-thud. . .thud-thud. . .rumble. . .thud-thud. . .thud-thud. . .rumble. . . Whatever it was grew closer. It chugged along slowly, its headlights illuminating the sand. Soon, the girls saw a big, yellow wall. They could almost touch the school bus as it lumbered by, and in the darkness, they could barely make out the words.

LASERS
LEVITATING
ELEVATING
WRIGHT &
SON
ORIENTEERING
RACING

"It's the Roswell bus," Bailey whispered. She and Sydney watched it disappear around the bend at the end of the road. "What do we do now?"

"Let's wait a few minutes," Sydney answered. "Until we're sure they're inside."

Soon the girls heard the sounds of hammering and sawing coming from the Wrights' place. Cautiously, they walked to the bend in the road and, keeping in the cover of the trees, they got close enough to see the Wrights' equipment shed. It was set about fifteen yards away from the grungy old house that Mr. Wright and Digger lived in.

The equipment shed was almost as big as the house, and its heavy front doors were wide open. A shower of sparks rained inside.

"Welding," said Sydney. "They must be working on the whatever-it-is."

An eerie, blue glow came from fluorescent lights hanging from the rafters, and a strong smell of hot steel wafted through the air.

The noise stopped for a few seconds. After a ghostly silence, the inside of the shed went dark.

"Look!" Bailey exclaimed. The shed lit up with flashing lights, first red, and then multicolored. "It's the spaceship. Remember? I said that they were reconstructing their ship from parts Digger found on the beach. Now do you believe me?"

Sydney had to admit that they were looking at

something very strange. "Let's get closer so we can see what's going on," she said.

"I wish we had that listening thing Kate has," said Bailey. "You know, that little gadget that lets you hear a conversation from a block away? Then we could know what's happening without having to go right to the building. Syd, do you think they have the lighthouse lady locked up in there?"

"I don't know," her friend replied. "But we're going to find out."

She took Bailey by the hand and they crept along the side of the road, careful to stay in the shadows. A soft whirring sound came from the shed now, and Sydney and Bailey made a wide circle, staying clear of the open doors. Then they tiptoed to the side of the shed, just below the window.

"I don't think it's safe to look inside just yet," Sydney said. "We should listen for a while."

She'd barely gotten the words out when the colored lights stopped and a bright white light started to flash. One, two, three, four, five flashes. Then nothing. One, two, three, four, five more.

"It's that code from *Close Encounters of the Third Kind*!" Bailey whispered. "That's the light we saw in the ocean yesterday morning."

The flashing stopped. For a few seconds, the shed went dark again. Then it was suddenly lit up by the overhead lights and the bluish fluorescent glow.

"Well, the signal lights work fine," the girls heard Digger say. "I wish I could program the other lights to change color so opponents can disguise themselves. It would add more strategy to the battle. Imagine that you're approaching a friendly craft, but when you get there, you find it's an enemy craft disguised as a friend."

The girls sat on the ground beneath the window with their backs pressed against the side of the building. Sydney could hear Bailey breathing fast and heavy. She felt her own muscles growing more tense.

Relax, Syd, she told herself. *Think! There has to be a logical explanation.*

Bailey whispered so softly that Sydney could barely hear her.

"Maybe they're not trying to get home to their planet," she said. "It sounds like they're going to wage war on an enemy spaceship, or something. Syd, they're planning a space war!"

"I doubt it, Bailey," Sydney whispered back. "You know at the lighthouse they said something about Captain Swain helping with the rudder. A rudder is part of a boat. Could that be some sort of funky boat?"

"That's a great idea," Mr. Wright boomed out. The girls jumped. Then as he continued, they realized he wasn't talking to them but to Digger. "But if I were you, son, I'd leave the lights alone for now. Save changing the colors for Phase Two. Hit 'em with what you've got. Then, after it takes off, surprise 'em with something even better."

"I guess you're right, Dad," said Digger.

"See? They're planning to strike with some sort of weapon," Bailey whispered. "It probably has to do with that coffee mug thing that we found on the beach."

Sydney was feeling very vulnerable sitting under the window. If anyone came along, they would surely see the girls. She noticed a brown tarp in the grass nearby. Staying close to the ground, she shimmied over and pulled it back to where Bailey sat.

"Here, let's cover up with this," she said, draping it over herself and Bailey.

"The noise problem is fixed now," Mr. Wright was saying. "When these crafts are on the ocean at night, the folks near the beach won't hear them. So there won't be any trouble."

"And I've got the hover fan working fine now," said Digger. "As soon as the craft hits the beach, a blast of air lifts it off the ground, and you can go anywhere without it being heard."

Bailey linked her arm with Sydney's.

"That was the puff of air that we felt on the beach!" she said. "Drake Wright went past us in the dark with that thing just a few yards away from us. Do you think he saw us?"

"I'm almost sure of it," Sydney answered. "Now we know the Wrights are responsible for those strange lights over the water."

"I'm telling you, it's a spacecraft!" Bailey insisted.

The word *hover* brought a picture in Sydney's mind.

"Listen, Bailey!" she exclaimed. "The word *hover*. . .one day at home, I thought I saw something just floating around outside my window. When I looked out, it was a remote-controlled helicopter one of my friends was flying. Do you think this is some sort of remote-controlled device? Like a spaceship-shaped, remote-controlled thing?"

"No. How could they fly it in the dark?" Bailey said.

"I'm going to text Kate," Sydney said, wiggling around to pull the phone out of her pocket. "She'll be able to tell us if it's at least possible."

Sydney had started texting when the sound of a hammer pounding against metal startled the girls. Digger said, "We need to get this rudder fixed. When that's done we can load her up."

The pounding started again.

"See, they do have the lighthouse lady," Bailey said. "I hope she's all right. They're planning to load her onto the spacecraft."

Sydney didn't answer. Her mind was racing trying to come up with answers for her questions. "*Test the spirits to see whether they are from God.*" She remembered hearing her pastor preach about that in church. As Sydney sat there thinking, she believed more than ever that Mr. Wright and Drake Wright were not space aliens.

"You know if it's some sort of boat—since rudders are part of boats—they always call boats 'she,' " Sydney explained.

"Cap has the paperwork done and everything is in order," Mr. Wright said. "It's up to you now, son. You have to get it out there for the right person to see. Plenty of investors are vacationing in Corolla and the other subdivisions around here. If you show it around, surely you'll find a backer or two."

"Huh?" Bailey whispered to Sydney under the tarp. "What are they talking about now?"

"Beats me," Sydney answered.

Listen, said a little voice in her head.

"We should just listen," she told Bailey.

"You have to get the word out," Mr. Wright continued. "I'm not going to help you this time, son. If you're going to be successful, you need to get out there with people and show them what you're up to. Why, think about our cousins. Some people thought they were crazy to keep jumping off cliffs with their flying machine, but they didn't let that get to them. They kept at it, and today—"

"But, Dad," Digger said, "I don't think I can do it. Besides, I don't mind keeping to myself. I like having time alone to wander and pick up stuff on the beach that we can sell to scrap yards. Last night, I found another doubloon for the Cap. He likes giving them to the kids at the lighthouse, you know."

The girls heard a few more strikes of the hammer against metal.

"Are you going to spend the rest of your life selling junk

you find on the beach?" Mr. Wright asked his son. "Or are you going to face your fear and live the life God gave you. Remember what the Cap always says."

"'I can do all things through Him who strengthens me,'" Digger replied.

"That's what Captain Swain said to me when I was afraid to climb the lighthouse," Bailey whispered.

"I know," Sydney answered. "I want to look inside and see what's going on."

"Me, too," Bailey said. "But I'm scared."

The girls stood, still wrapped in the tarp. They dropped it around their shoulders and peeked through the dirty window.

"Oh my." Bailey gasped.

"Awesome," Sydney exclaimed in a whisper.

In the center of the shed sat a vehicle beyond her imagination. It was about the size of a small car, but round. It was painted a soft gray-blue, the color of the ocean on an overcast day. The paint sparkled the way sunlight dances on waves.

In the center of the craft a cockpit was covered with a clear glass bubble. It reminded Sydney of pictures she'd seen in school textbooks of fighter jets. As she watched, Digger climbed into the cockpit and flipped a switch. The flashing colored lights encircled the craft and spun around its middle. Drake Wright sat in the driver's seat and grinned.

"What do you think it is?" Bailey asked.

"I don't know," Sydney replied. "It's not like anything I've seen in my whole life. It's kind of beautiful."

"But scary, too," Bailey added.

"Maybe it wouldn't be if we knew what it was," said Sydney.

A muted *whoosh* came from the craft. It sounded like a choir softly singing "Shhhhhh. . ."

As Bailey and Sydney watched, the machine rose off the ground. It hovered several feet above the floor. Then it slowly began to rotate. It spun around faster and faster, and the girls heard Digger laughing gleefully. Slowly, it stopped and dropped gently back to the floor. Drake opened the cover on the cockpit and said, "Well, if it doesn't make it as a water sport, maybe I can market it as a carnival ride."

Mr. Wright chuckled. "You're a Wright, my boy," he said. "You always have a backup plan."

Sydney motioned to Bailey to sit. The girls sank back to the ground and covered themselves with the tarp.

"Now I'm really confused," said Bailey. "I'm not so sure it's a spaceship anymore, are you?"

"I was never sure it was a spaceship," said Sydney. "I just don't know what it is yet."

She started to crawl out from under the tarp again.

"What are you doing now?" Bailey asked.

"Stay put," Sydney answered. She crawled to the window. When she was sure the Wrights had their backs to her, she took several photos of the contraption. Then she climbed back under the tarp.

"I didn't use the flash," she said. "I think it's bright enough in there for the pictures to turn out." She looked at the display on her phone and saw she was right. The photos were clear enough to show the craft in the middle of the equipment shed floor.

"Now what?" Bailey asked.

"I'm texting Kate," Sydney replied. "And sending her these pictures. You know how smart she is about technological stuff. She might know what this is."

SYDNEY: K8, WE'RE HIDING OUT NEXT TO THE WRIGHTS' EQUIPMENT SHED. LOOK AT THESE PICTURES. THEY'VE BUILT THIS THING. IT HAS FLASHING LIGHTS THAT SPIN AROUND IT. IT CAN HOVER A FEW FEET OFF THE FLOOR AND IT ROTATES REALLY FAST. WHAT IS IT?

Sydney sent the message, flipped her phone closed, and stuck it back in her pocket.

"I don't think the Wrights are aliens," she told Bailey. "It looks like that thing is just another one of their crazy inventions. But what is it?"

"Digger said something about a water sport," said Bailey.

"I don't think a water sport would be remote-controlled," Sydney said reluctantly. "And we'll wait to hear back from Kate, but I think anything that is as big as that would be too heavy to be remote-controlled. . ."

"Unless the battery was as big as a bus!" Bailey said.

"Hmm. Could they have a giant battery in that bus of theirs?" Sydney asked. "Nah. I don't think that's the answer."

"But they talked about battles and enemies. That doesn't fit with any water sport I know of. And what about the lighthouse lady? Where has she disappeared to? And then there's Captain Swain. Who do you think he *really* is? And where is he? Wasn't he supposed to be here helping the Wrights tonight?"

"I'm right here, Bailey Chang," said a voice in the darkness. "And I can answer all of your questions."

CHAPTER 11

Answers

Bailey and Sydney crawled out from under the tarp.

Captain Swain stood in the shadows looking at them. He was still wearing jeans, as he had been that morning, and now he had on a sweatshirt that said NAVY on its front. His captain's cap sat squarely on his head.

"What are you girls doing here?" he asked gently.

"You answer our question first," said Bailey. "Who are you, really?"

"You know who I am, Bailey Chang," said the captain. "I'm Captain Nathan Swain."

"No, you're not!" Sydney answered. "Captain Nathan Swain is dead. We saw his picture in an old paper. He was the lighthouse keeper here about a hundred years ago, so you can't be him unless you're an imposter."

"Or a ghost!" Bailey added.

"Well, I don't think you're a ghost," Sydney said with a smile. "But Captain Nathan Swain, the lighthouse keeper, didn't have any sons, so you can't be his son. But I suspect you're another relative."

The captain smiled. "Kudos. Congratulations to you for figuring it out, Miss Sydney Lincoln. Captain Nathan Swain, the lighthouse keeper, was my uncle," he said. "I resemble him, but I can assure you, Miss Bailey Chang, that I'm *not* his ghost. Now, as far as being an imposter, Sydney Lincoln, I'll admit to that. I sometimes masquerade as my uncle."

"Why?" Sydney asked.

Before the captain could answer, Bailey interrupted.

"If you're for real, why did you disappear when we were at the top of the lighthouse?" She climbed out from the tarp and stood up. "One minute you were there, and then you were gone. And the same thing happened on the beach. You were there walking your dog, we talked to you, and then you disappeared. What's up with that?"

The captain leaned against the side of the equipment shed.

"Bailey, my girl, you have quite the imagination. I'm sorry if you thought I had abandoned you. Once you girls were safe on the lookout, I hurried to an appointment I was already late for. I should have said farewell, at least. I sincerely apologize for being rude." He tipped the brim of his cap. "As for the incident on the beach, McTavish saw a cat and ran off. I ran after him. McTavish is a good boy, you know, but he hates cats and would do harm to one if he caught it. I'm sure by the time you looked for me, I was chasing my dog across the dunes."

The clues were beginning to add up for Sydney. There

was no ghost of Captain Nathan Swain, and she was certain the captain wasn't helping the Wrights build a spaceship.

"But you were wearing a captain's uniform at the lighthouse," she said, getting off the ground. "The kind captains wore years and years ago."

"I was acting," said the captain. "I volunteer at the lighthouse where I play the role of Captain Nathan Swain, the lighthouse keeper. When schoolchildren tour, I tell them the story of the lighthouse and about the pirates and shipwrecks of the Outer Banks. In fact, years ago, I *did* work in the lighthouse, helping maintain the beacon up top."

Bailey was beginning to feel a bit foolish for thinking that the captain was a ghost, but she still had some unanswered questions.

"So why were you on the beach yesterday morning with Digger?" she asked. "We heard you talking with him about not putting *the vehicle* in the water until after I went home. What exactly is he up to, and what's that thing in the shed?"

The captain shook his head. "'Let the words of my mouth be acceptable in Your sight, O Lord. . .' Just me and God talking out loud," he said. "I know that folks around here call him Digger, but Drake Wright is the young man's name. And, Bailey, before I tell you what young Mr. Wright and I were discussing yesterday morning, why don't you tell me why you girls are hiding here in the dark."

Bailey sighed. She was almost certain her theory about space aliens and space wars was wrong. "We thought. . .

well, actually *I* thought the Wrights were space aliens and you were helping them get back to the Mother Ship after their spacecraft crashed into the ocean. I thought Digger, I mean Drake, was picking up pieces of the spacecraft along the beach and that the Wrights were rebuilding it in their equipment shed. And I think they've kidnapped the lighthouse lady. I thought they were going to take her to wherever with them. We're spying on them to find out what's going on."

The captain chuckled. "And you, Miss Lincoln, do you believe in aliens from outer space?"

"I guess I always thought there was a logical explanation," Sydney said. "But I agree with Bailey that a lot of things are happening that just don't add up. Why did you and the Wrights put a telescope on the lighthouse lookout this morning?"

The captain chuckled again. "That telescope is part of the lighthouse renovation. It's there so visitors can view the ocean from the tower. And, Bailey Chang, the lighthouse lady—I assume you mean the young woman who works at the lighthouse and is named Meghan Kent, by the way. She's—"

"Wait, don't tell me," Sydney said. "She's just taking a day off and when the Wrights were referring to 'she' they meant their invention."

"Again, cheers to you, Sydney Lincoln," said Captain Swain. "Miss Meghan Kent is on vacation for a few days while some remodeling takes place. People who are vacationing here don't stop to think that sometimes we natives need vacations ourselves!"

The captain paused and smiled at the girls.

"Come on inside," said the captain. "There are a couple of fellows I'd like you to meet."

The girls walked with Captain Swain around the side of the equipment shed and through the open front doors. Drake turned and greeted the captain with a smile, but when he saw the girls, his smile faded. "Oh," he said, softly.

Mr. Wright walked toward them wiping his hands on a rose-colored rag.

"Hi, Cap." He greeted his friend with a handshake. "I see you've brought some visitors." His voice held a hint of disapproval, and his blue eyes flashed at Sydney and then at Bailey.

"It's all right, Nate," said the captain. "These are my friends and they can be trusted. This is Sydney Lincoln and Bailey Chang." His right hand swept toward the girls.

"You're the kid who looked at me through the lighthouse window this morning," Mr. Wright said gruffly.

"I'm sorry, Mr. Wright," Bailey apologized.

"The girls have been watching us test Drake's invention, and they're curious to know more about it," the captain said.

Sydney noticed that Drake's face had turned a bright shade of red. He looked shyly down at his feet as he stood next to the mysterious craft. Sydney walked up to him with a smile, "Hi, Drake," she said, extending her hand. "It's very nice to meet you."

Drake Wright looked up, but not directly into Sydney's eyes. He grasped the tips of her fingers, gave them a little shake, and then dropped his hand to his side. "I've seen you around," he mumbled.

"Drake, why don't you tell the girls about the Wright D-94 Wave Smasher?" said the captain. "It's okay to talk about it now. You own the patent. I have the paperwork to prove it."

Drake swallowed hard. He looked more embarrassed than ever.

"Go on, son," Mr. Wright encouraged him. "Tell them what this is."

"Yeah," Bailey said, stroking the shiny blue paint. "We can't wait to know."

When Drake saw Bailey's hand touch the paint on the D-94, he stopped looking embarrassed. "Please don't touch it," he said firmly.

Bailey quickly pulled her hand away and stepped backward. "Why? What's it going to do?"

"It's not going to do anything," Drake answered. He pulled a rag out of the back pocket of his blue jeans and polished the spot Bailey had touched. "I just finished waxing it."

"Oh," said Bailey.

"So tell us about this," Sydney said. She walked around the craft so she could see it from all sides. "You were talking about a rudder. Let me guess. This is a new form of transportation."

Drake said nothing.

"'I can do all things through Him who strengthens me,'" Captain Swain said. "Just me and God talking, Drake." He walked over to the young man and put his arm around his shoulder. "Think of this as a rehearsal. Tell them about the next great Wright invention, the one that's destined to change life on the Outer Banks forever."

Drake looked at his feet for a few seconds. Then he took a deep breath and began what sounded like a well-rehearsed speech. "This is a vehicle called the Wright D-94 Wave Smasher. It's a new recreational water vehicle that I've been working on for the past several years. The D-94 is unlike any other recreational water vehicle because it can ride on the water or sail up to thirty feet above it with the flick of a switch. It's built tough enough to withstand a ten-foot wave, and the driver is completely protected in the cockpit, so he won't get hurt or wet."

"Or *she*," Bailey corrected him. "Girls can use it, too, right?"

When Bailey saw Drake's shy smile she was positive that he fell into the "cute" category.

"Yes, girls can use it, too," Drake answered. "But it's not a toy. It's for professional sportsmen—I mean sports people," he corrected himself.

"So why did you invent it?" Sydney asked.

"Well," Drake went on, "you can travel up and down the Outer Banks and see all sorts of fun things to do on the water. You can kite sail, hang glide, water ski, kayak, sail a boat. . .there are all kinds of activities. But there's nothing like the D-94. In the daytime, it's a superfast racing boat. You can zoom across the water, leap over waves, and even hover or sail up to thirty feet above the water. In fact, it even works on the beach. You just press a button, and it becomes a hover craft that rides on a cushion of air, or it can walk on its feet." He pushed a button, and four tennis-racket shaped platforms came out of the bottom of the craft.

"So *you* made those strange footprints and passed us on the beach," said Sydney. "You scared us half to death."

"Sorry about that." Drake smiled. "But I didn't think anyone would be out that early in the morning. I've had to be real careful so no one stole my idea until Cap here got me the patent."

"So you only tested it at night?" Bailey asked.

"Yeah," Drake answered. "But there's a reason for that. That D-94 is not only a daytime recreational water vehicle, it's actually a very expensive game piece."

"Huh?" asked Sydney.

"Well, you see," Drake said. "I've also invented a new water sport." He walked over to one wall of the equipment shed and pointed to a big drawing on a sheet of paper stuck to the wall. "Come over here," he said.

When the girls got closer, they saw the drawing looked like a football field off the shore of the ocean. There were pictures of D-94s positioned on the field and a goal post on either end.

"I don't have a catchy name for it yet," said Drake, "but it's all done with lights. Players compete on teams, and the goal is to get all your D-94s safely into your end zone. You play in the dark on an imaginary field on the ocean. A floating string of lights outlines both end zones. The only other lights are on the D-94s. The lights can be stationary or flashing, and they're used as a way to signal plays to other members of your team."

"Baseball players use hand signals, and in this game, the players use light signals instead," said Sydney.

"Yeah, that's right," Drake said, looking like his confidence was growing.

"Wow, this is so cool!" said Sydney. Just then, her cell phone started to vibrate. She excused herself, flipped open the phone, and found a message from Kate. I THINK IT LOOKS TOO HEAVY TO BE A REMOTE-CONTROL DEVICE. I GOOGLED NATE WRIGHT. HE HAS A REPUTATION FOR CREATIVE FORMS OF TRANSPORTATION, SO I WOULD GUESS THAT IT'S AN EXPERIMENT THAT HAS SOMETHING TO DO WITH THAT. INVENTORS ARE OFTEN HUSH-HUSH UNTIL THEY HAVE THE KINKS OF THEIR EXPERIMENTS WORKED OUT AND UNTIL THEY GET A PATENT. B CAREFUL! K8

Sydney texted back: YOU'RE RIGHT. IT'S A WRIGHT D-94 WAVE SMASHER. MORE LATER.

"Can you imagine how awesome a game would look from the beach?" Bailey asked. "With all those lights scooting around and flying over the water?"

"I can," Sydney answered. "It was pretty exciting when we thought your D-94 was a UFO. People are going to love watching these things at night."

Mr. Wright was standing near his son, grinning. "And Drake here has taken extra-special care to make sure that it runs quietly so it doesn't disturb the residents. They already think we're crazy, you know. They don't get it that some of the craziest-looking ideas might change the world someday."

"Like the Wright Brothers' flying machine," said Bailey.

"That's *right*!" said Captain Swain. Everyone laughed. "Girls," he said with a serious tone. "Always remember: 'Do not judge according to appearance, but judge with righteous judgement.' That's just me and God talking to you," he said.

"You like to quote God, don't you?" said Sydney.

"I do," the captain replied. "His Bible gives me the words, and I just speak them aloud."

"Just like our friend Bettyboo," Bailey answered. "She likes to quote scripture verses, too." She walked over and stood next to Drake. He was about a foot taller than she was, and he had deep brown eyes. She was happy that he

141

finally looked at her instead of down at his feet. "What are your plans for the D-94?" she asked.

Drake clammed up again, and his face turned red. Sydney noticed that he looked very uncomfortable. "Drake, I'm sorry for not getting to know you sooner, and even sorrier that I was suspicious of you and your dad."

"Me, too," Bailey agreed. "I guess I let my imagination get the best of me."

Nate Wright took off his cap and scratched his head. "Imagination isn't a bad thing," he said. "Don't be sorry for letting it go when it wants to run, but remember that you have to reign it in once in a while. Otherwise, it *will* get the best of you."

"I'll remember, Mr. Wright," Bailey said. "So, how about it, Drake, what are you going to do with the D-94?"

Drake sat on some tires stacked in a corner of the shed. "Well," he said. "Dad and the captain think I need to promote it. You know, get it out there in the ocean in the daytime and show it off. They both think people are living in Corolla Light who have the money to back my invention and get it into the hands of the right people."

"Like companies that build recreational water vehicles and race boats and stuff?" Sydney asked. An idea was beginning to form in her head.

"Yeah, exactly," Drake replied. "Know anybody?"

It was a rhetorical question. He didn't really expect an answer, but Sydney had one for him.

"Mr. Kessler," she said.

"Who?" Mr. Wright asked.

"The Kessler twins' dad," said Sydney. "They have a house near my grandparents' place. Mr. Kessler runs a company that builds race boats and other water vehicles. I'm sure he'd be interested in seeing the Wright D-94 Wave Smasher."

"'God works for the good of those who love Him,'" said Captain Swain, smiling. "Where can we find Mr. Kessler?"

"They're in the Village at the crab fest," said Bailey. "The whole family is there. I think we should all go over there and find them, before the crab boil and all the stuff that goes with it is eaten up."

"And if you want an audience at the beach when you show off your invention, you only have to tell the Kessler twins about it. They're terrible at keeping secrets," said Sydney.

The Wrights washed up in an old sink in the equipment shed while the girls and the captain waited.

"I have a couple more questions, if you don't mind," said Bailey.

"Go ahead," Mr. Wright told her.

"Well, are the words on your bus a secret code?"

"Bailey!" Sydney scolded.

"Why would you even think that?" asked Drake.

Bailey felt a little embarrassed, but she wanted answers. "If you read the first letters of the words backward they spell *Roswell*, like that place in New Mexico where the spaceship crashed back in 1947. I thought maybe your invention was a UFO."

Drake laughed out loud.

"Okay, call me silly," said Bailey. "But what is that weird coffee mug that lights up inside. We heard you say that it belongs to you. I thought it was an alien weapon."

Drake looked at her wide-eyed. "A what! It's no weapon. It's my idea for a pinhole flashlight that's magnetically powered," he said. "It's another invention I'm working on. I'm hoping someday it'll be a fun thing for kids to use when they go ghost-crab hunting."

"Okay," Bailey said, slapping him on the shoulder. "You've passed the Camp Club Girls' interrogation. You and your dad are definitely *not* from outer space. Now, let's go find the Kesslers."

The Wright D-94 Wave Smasher

Hi, Camp Club Girls.

Well, last night, at the Wrights' equipment shed, we solved the mysteries of the UFO and Captain Swain. The Wrights aren't space aliens, and Captain Swain isn't a ghost.

Drake has invented an awesome water vehicle called the wright D-94 Wave Smasher (pictures attached). That's what we've seen over the water at night. He's been testing it. It's also what made the footprints on the beach and whooshed by us that day. Captain Swain helped Drake get a patent on it. The D-94 can race like a speedboat, jump waves, and hover or fly about 30 feet over the water. And Drake invented a new water sport to go with it. He doesn't have a name for it yet, but it's played in the dark, and the lights on the vehicle have a lot to do with the strategy of how its played.

Drake is really shy (Bailey says to tell you he's really cute, too). He was nervous about showing his invention to anyone. We convinced him he has to or else he'll never sell it and become famous like his distant cousins the Wright Brothers. So tonight he'll demonstrate the wave smasher at the beach. One of our neighbors runs a company that makes racing boats. I introduced him to Drake last night, and he can't wait to see the D-94 in action. Bailey and I are going to the beach now to watch.

That's all we know. Mystery solved. The only question that's still hanging out there is: What really happened to the sailors on the Carroll A. Deering? *Nobody knows for sure. Maybe you guys can all come here next summer, and we can crack that case together.*

All for now,
Sydney

P.S. from Bailey: I'm really sorry that I called Drake "Digger." The captain said, "Do not judge according to appearances, but judge with righteous judgement." I think Drake Wright and his dad are awesome! Oh, and we forgot to tell you, Captain Swain is the nephew of the Old Captain Swain, the

*lighthouse keeper. He dresses like the old
captain when he volunteers at the lighthouse.
Syd says to tell you the lighthouse lady is on
vacation. Aliens did not abduct her.*

Sydney put her binoculars and cell phone into her backpack, zipped it shut, and slung it over her shoulder. "Let's go," she said to Bailey.

Bailey went into the bathroom to check herself out in the mirror. She smoothed her straight, black hair and applied strawberry lip gloss to her thin, pale lips. "Can I use some of your banana-coconut body spray?" she asked Sydney.

"Sure," Sydney agreed.

Bailey spritzed some onto her arms and her neck. "So, do you think he's going to buy it?" she asked.

"Who?" Sydney wondered.

"Do you think that the twins' dad is going to buy Drake's idea?"

"I really think he might," Sydney answered. "He sure liked the Wave Smasher when he saw it in the Wrights' equipment shed, and since we gave the twins the job of spreading the word around Corolla, I think people will come out to see it."

Bailey took one last look in the mirror. Then she picked up her backpack and slipped her arms through its straps. "Okay, let's go," she said.

At twilight, the girls walked down the beach to Tuna Street. A crowd was starting to gather. Families spread blankets in the sand and sipped bottles of water. Several big floodlights were there to illuminate the beach, and a small set of bleachers was set up for special guests who might want to buy Drake's invention. The Wrights' bus was parked at the end of the access road. Drake, his dad, and the captain were rolling the D-94 out of a trailer that was hitched onto the back bumper. When Captain Swain saw the girls, he tipped the brim of his cap. "Good evening, young ladies," he said.

"Hi, Captain. Hi, Drake!" Bailey said, brightly.

"Hi," Drake responded without looking up.

"A lot of people are here," Sydney said as she noticed more curious onlookers arriving in cars, on bikes, and on foot. Several men in business suits, looking quite out of place, stood at the end of Tuna Street talking with Mr. Kessler. "I guess Carolyn and Marilyn got busy getting the word out."

"I guess *so*," Drake replied.

Bailey saw that he seemed nervous. "Hey, just imagine you're one of the Wright brothers," she said. "I'm sure they drew a big crowd with their flying machine. It's your turn now, Drake. Trust me. They'll love you."

The corners of Drake's lips curled into a tiny smile. "I don't want them to love me," he said. "I just want them to love my D-94."

"That, too!" said Bailey.

"My boy," the captain said. "This is your shining moment. I don't think we should just launch the craft without a fanfare. Why, when they launch a ship there are speeches, and sometimes they even smash a bottle on the bow—"

"I don't want anything smashed on my invention!" Drake exclaimed.

"No, no, I didn't mean that." The captain chuckled. "I just think that we should make this an occasion. Do you still have that megaphone in the bus?"

Drake's face turned beet red.

"It's under the driver's seat," Mr. Wright said. "I agree with you, Cap. We should make this special."

Drake gulped. "Do I have to do all the talking? I mean do I have to tell everybody about my invention?"

"No," said the captain. "I'll introduce you as the inventor and give a brief account of what you are about to show them. I think, for now, we should keep the water sport part to ourselves. That's something that you can discuss privately with Mr. Kessler and his friends. You can meet with them after the demonstration and answer their questions."

The captain went to the bus to get the megaphone.

By now, the crowd was trying to push toward the Wrights to get a better look at the shiny machine. "Get back, please!" Nate Wright shouted. Everyone took a giant step backward. Before long, the beach security team showed up and stretched a line of yellow tape between two posts that they pounded into the sand. They patrolled the line, telling onlookers to stay behind the line. The Kessler twins showed up, and the officers let them through.

"We told security that they'd better get down here," said Carolyn.

"We told them to hurry, because we needed crowd control," Marilyn added. "Tons of people are here already!"

The only time Sydney had seen the beach more packed was on the Fourth of July. "How many people did you tell?" she asked.

"Hundreds!" said Carolyn.

"At least!" added Marilyn. "When we got home from the crab fest last night, we printed up flyers on our computer. We told everyone to come down here at eight o'clock tonight because a UFO was going to be on the beach."

"We used up two big packs of paper—" said Carolyn.

"And a whole black ink cartridge," said Marilyn. "Then we got up early this morning and started putting them in all the mailboxes."

"And after that, we went to the shopping centers," said Carolyn. "And we stuck flyers under the windshield wipers of all the cars in the parking lots."

"But then a guy came out and told us not to do it anymore, so we left," said Marilyn.

Captain Swain stepped out of the bus with the megaphone in his hand. He turned it on and pointed it toward the crowd. "Testing one, two, three, four. Testing." His deep voice boomed across the beach. He turned the megaphone off.

"I thought you didn't like crowds, Captain," Sydney said.

"I don't," the captain replied. "But this is an historical day. Why, once people see the Wrights as serious twenty-first-century inventors, we can only imagine how their inventions will someday change the world."

As twilight faded to darkness, Mr. Kessler and his friends ducked under the yellow tape. The twins' dad wore khaki shorts, a white tee shirt, and flip-flops. His friends were obviously not as prepared for the beach. They had taken off their suit coats, rolled their pants legs above their knees, and were barefoot. "Let's get this show on the road," Mr. Kessler said. "Are you ready, Drake?"

"Yes, sir," Drake replied.

Mr. Kessler and his friends joined several others who were seated on the bleachers.

Bailey was at Drake's side now. She stood on her tiptoes and whispered to him. "You can do it. Just keep repeating to yourself, 'I can do all things through Him who strengthens me.' That's what I did when I climbed the lighthouse."

Drake's face turned redder than ever.

The captain flipped a switch inside the bus, and floodlights wired from the bus turned the beach from darkness to daylight. He then walked to the front of the crowd and stood with the megaphone in his hands. "Ladies and gentlemen, boys and girls, may I please have your undivided attention?"

A hush fell over the crowd.

"I have the great privilege of introducing one of our own, Mr. Drake Wright!" He swept his left hand toward Drake.

Bailey, Sydney, and the twins moved out of the way, leaving Drake by himself next to the Wright D-94 Wave Smasher. They began to clap loudly.

"Let's hear it for Drake!" Bailey shouted. Then everyone on the beach clapped and cheered.

The captain continued, "Drake and his dad, Nate Wright, are well known around Corolla as inventors, and tonight Drake will show you an invention he has worked on tirelessly for the past several years. It is a recreational watercraft unlike anything you have ever seen. As soon as you have watched it in action, you will want a Wright D-94 Wave Smasher of your very own. I won't take up your valuable time explaining the fine points of his amazing invention. I will, instead, let it speak for itself. Drake, my boy, take it away!"

Drake climbed into the cockpit and pulled down the bubble-like cover. He started the engine and the soft whirring sound began. He pushed a button making the four snowshoe-like feet pop out of the bottom of the vehicle. Then another button raised the D-94 up on its legs. It started walking toward the water, and people in the crowd gasped.

"You haven't seen anything yet, ladies and gentlemen," the captain said. "Prepare to be amazed."

When Drake got within several feet of the water, he let the D-94 lift and hover a few yards above the beach. Then it started rotating.

"It walks. It hovers. It even spins!" the captain announced. "Around and around she goes!"

Drake let his invention spin faster and faster until it looked like a top spinning out of control. The crowd oohed and aahed. Then, slowly, Drake let the craft rotate counterclockwise to a complete stop. He set it down in the ocean, just offshore. The legs and feet folded up into the bottom of the vehicle and it floated.

"How about a game of leapfrog?" the captain asked the crowd.

With the spotlights fixed on his craft, Drake pushed the control stick forward, and the D-94 sailed out to sea, leaping over waves that got in its way. The crowd went wild. Captain Swain flicked a switch, and all the spotlights went dark. "Keep your eyes fixed on the horizon," the captain said. "The best is yet to come."

"Now what?" Carolyn asked in the darkness.

"Yeah, now what?" Marilyn repeated.

"Just watch," Sydney answered. "He'll make it look like a UFO."

"He's so awesome," Bailey remarked. "He can make the D-94 do just about anything."

Offshore, Drake turned on the signal light. It flashed bright white in a series of dots and dashes. "He says, 'Watch this, Dad,'" Sydney heard Mr. Wright say as he stood nearby. "I'm so proud of you, son," Mr. Wright said, although Drake couldn't hear him.

The Wright D-94 Wave Smasher lit up like a Christmas tree, first with red lights chasing around its middle, then with multicolored lights flashing on and off. As the crowd watched, Drake made the craft shoot like a bullet across the water. Its lights provided the only clue as to where it was. To make things even more interesting, Drake sometimes turned off all the lights and then changed places before turning them back on.

"He's over there!" someone in the crowd shouted.

"No, he's over there!"

"Look at how fast that thing can move."

"You can't tell if it's on or above the water!"

Drake put on an amazing show before bringing the craft back to shore. As he approached the beach, Captain Swain flipped the spotlights back on. The D-94 sailed to the water's edge and lifted off the sand with a puff of air. It scooted across the beach to where the bus was parked, and then Drake set it down to rest in the sand. He killed the engine and pulled back the cover on the cockpit.

"That was more wonderful than anything I could ever

have imagined," said Bailey.

"Wow, that's saying a lot," Sydney replied. "You have the wildest imagination of anyone I've ever known."

"Ladies and gentlemen," the captain shouted. "Let's give a big round of applause to our resident inventor, *Mr. Drake Wright*!"

Everyone on the beach applauded, and many tried to get past the yellow tape. "Stay back!" Mr. Wright shouted.

"That's all for tonight," the captain announced. "There will be plenty more opportunities for you to see the Wright D-94 Wave Smasher in action. And before long, you might even have one of your very own." He shut off the megaphone and climbed down the ladder.

"Drake," Captain Swain said, approaching the D-94, "you were incredible!"

"Yes, you were!" Bailey agreed.

"We think so, too," said Carolyn and Marilyn.

Drake climbed out of the cockpit, and Sydney shook his hand.

"You did that just like a pro," she said. "I was praying for you the whole time."

"Thanks, Sydney," Drake said with a lot more confidence in his voice. "I felt your prayers. I couldn't have done it without you guys—"

"And the Greatest Helper of them all," said the captain, pointing up at the sky.

"He means God," Sydney whispered to the twins.

Mr. Kessler had climbed down from the bleachers and was walking toward them.

"Here comes our dad," said Marilyn.

"Drake." Mr. Kessler said in a serious voice. "My associates and I would like to have a word with you and your dad. Over there, please." He motioned to the bleachers where his friends were waiting. The Wrights followed Mr. Kessler through the sand.

"What do you think will happen?" Sydney asked.

"They're going to set him up," Carolyn said.

"Huh?" said Bailey.

"We overheard our dad talking on the phone this morning," said Marilyn. "He said that if Drake's demonstration went well tonight, his company will start manufacturing the Wright D-94 Wave Smasher."

"And there's more," said Carolyn. "He's going to set up a dealership, right here in Corolla, and Drake's dad will run it, and everybody on the Outer Banks will come here to buy their D-94s."

"Before long, there will be dealerships up and down both coasts," Marilyn added. "And Drake and his dad will own them all."

Captain Swain beamed. "Praise our God! His deeds are wonderful, too marvelous to describe."

"You really need to meet our friend Beth," Sydney told him. "You two could have a contest to see who knows the most scripture verses."

"Why, Sydney Lincoln," said Captain Swain, "I'd be honored to meet your friend. Maybe she can come with you the next time you visit your grandparents."

A few yards away from them, they heard Drake Wright let out a joyful whoop! Mr. Wright threw his arms around his son and hugged him.

"Watch that boy," said the captain. "This is only the beginning."